Little, Brown and Company
Hachette Book Group
1290 Avenue of the Americas, New York, NY 10104
Visit us at lb-kids.com

Little, Brown and Company is a division of Hachette Book Group, Inc.
The Little, Brown name and logo are trademarks of Hachette Book Group, Inc.

The publisher is not responsible for websites (or their content) that
are not owned by the publisher.

First Edition: November 2016

Paperback ISBN: 978-0-316-35680-0
Paper over board ISBN: 978-0-316-39394-2

Library of Congress Control Number: 2016939832

10 9 8 7 6 5 4 3 2 1

LSC-C

Printed in the United States of America

Ever After High™

Epic Winter

The Junior Novel

by *Perdita Finn*

Based on the screenplay written by Nina Bargiel, Sherry Klein,
MJ Offen, Audu Paden, and Keith Wagner

LITTLE, BROWN AND COMPANY
New York Boston

CHAPTER 1

Summer's Almost Over

*O*nce upon a time in the land of fairytales," began Brooke Page's mother.

Brooke peered over her mother's shoulder at the vivid picture of the Ever After High castle. This was the boarding school where the children of princesses and evil witches and fairytale characters of all kinds went to find their destinies— or, if possible, to change them. The sun was shining on the gleaming turrets. Students were hurrying to class with their friends. They wore flowy dresses and shorts. They were sipping lemonade. Beads of sweat dotted their foreheads. They were hot; it was summer.

But the picture didn't match the story.

"Brr," Brooke's father read. *"An icy, freezing adventure was about to begin."*

Brooke's mother continued. *"A chilling quest in which our heroes must face the cold of an unrelenting winter..."*

"Brave the icy blasts of treacherous snowstorms..."

"Whoa, whoa, whoa," interrupted Brooke. "Mom. Dad. I think you are confused." She brushed a strand of long dark hair out of her eyes as she studied the picture in the fairytale book. "Here at Ever After High, it's summer. Look!"

Brooke's father nodded. "That's right, Brooke. Down there." Then he pointed to a faraway spot in the picture. "But up here at the top of the world, it's always winter."

Brooke peered at the blur of white nestled in the corner of the image. She could make out clouds and the barest outline of an ice castle, covered in snow.

"Behold the Ice Castle of the Royal Winter Family," announced Brooke's mom. *"Who control and protect all things frosty!"*

"I think you'd better back up a few pages," decided Brooke. "This I gotta see."

Brooke's mother flipped backward in the book to a picture of a large, snow-covered gate. It was time for Brooke to meet the Snow Queen and the Snow King at last!

CHAPTER 2

A Blast of Cold Air

The Snow King and the Snow Queen looked out from the castle balcony at their sparkling white kingdom. Icicles hung from the railing. The air was frosty and clear. The Snow Queen leaned against her husband. He wrapped an arm around her. They smiled at each other. The Snow King rubbed his nose affectionately against the Snow Queen's.

"Ew!" exclaimed Crystal Winter, their daughter. She'd come out to join them. "Save the snuggling for the fireside."

Her parents turned to gaze happily at their daughter. She was holding a pair of skates in her hand.

"Let's play some indoor ice hockey," Crystal suggested.

"I'm up for that!" The Snow King grinned. He held up his royal scepter—and it turned into a hockey stick made out of ice. "My queen? Will you referee?"

The queen nodded. She blew on a whistle she wore around her neck.

The king walked into the throne room and tapped the marble floor with his hockey stick. Instantly, the floor turned to ice. He banged on it again, and a perfectly formed rink rose up around it. They were ready to play.

As soon as Crystal got her skates laced, that was. The palace pixies were giving her a hand.

Her mother shook her head. "If you're going to rule one day, it's high time you lace your own skates."

"But we have pixies for that," protested Crystal. She stood up. "C'mon, Mom, it's game time."

The Snow King and Crystal skated to the center of the rink. They faced each other, their hockey sticks poised and ready. The Snow Queen blew into her hand and formed a solid-ice hockey puck. She dropped it between the two players and whistled again. *Let the game begin!*

Both Crystal and her dad were expert skaters—gliding, turning, swooping in with their sticks to catch the puck. The Snow King scooped the puck forward and sped after it toward the goal. Crystal raced after him.

From the sidelines, frost elves, the loyal subjects of the king and queen, cheered with delight. The palace pixies giggled and clapped. But no one noticed as two snowy owls glided into the room, one of them holding a small envelope in his beak. No one noticed as they landed silently in the back row and folded their wings. And no one noticed as they magically transformed into frost elves. Jackie Frost, a royal teen rebel, scowled at the good-natured antics of the royal family on ice. Her sibling sidekick, Northwind, was still holding the envelope in his mouth.

"Look at those overgrown royal penguins," sneered Jackie. "Northwind, hand me our secret weapon."

Northwind opened his mouth, and the envelope fluttered into Jackie's hands. "What's the next move?" Northwind asked.

Jackie was scowling. "All that power and what do they do with it? Have fun? Bleh. They deserve to have it stolen."

She opened the envelope, and whatever was inside it glowed a deep and devious purple.

"Careful, Jackie! That's pure evil," Northwind warned.

"No duh! How else are we supposed to take over? By asking nicely? Sheesh. How many times do I have to explain the plan to you?"

Northwind blinked. "One more?"

"We turn the sweet Snow King sour," she said with a sigh. "Then he'll start the most wicked winter ever after. Crystal isn't ready to rule—she won't be able to take the heat. So once she's out of the picture, we save the day from the crazy king, and before you know it, rule of the season will belong to *me*!" She cleared her throat as she noticed the confused expression on Northwind's face. "Us. Whatever," she corrected.

With a whirl of ice dust, Crystal and the Snow King whizzed past Northwind and Jackie Frost. They were laughing as they stole the puck back and forth from each other.

The Snow King was about to score, but at the last possible moment, Crystal spun around and used her magical hockey stick to create an ice arch over her father's head—leading to the opposite goal. She glided down it on her skates and shot the puck toward the net.

Score! The crowd cheered and the Snow King congratulated his daughter. "Well played, kiddo!" She was the best—and he had taught her.

The Snow Queen frowned. "She can't just magic her way out of everything, dear."

"Why not?" The Snow King laughed. "Works for me!" He blew his wife a kiss, and it froze into the shape of a heart in midair before landing on her cheek. The Snow Queen blushed.

"Mom! Dad! Cut out the slushy stuff!" Crystal scolded her parents.

CHAPTER 3

Bad Weather

They were a happy family. Together, they gazed out at their frosty kingdom from the balcony of the castle. The Snow King waved his scepter, and a light snow began to fall gently.

The Snow King wrapped an arm around his daughter. "Your mother's right," he said gently. "Life can't be all fun and games. One day, you'll rule winter."

"But I am ready to rule," Crystal protested. "I've read every magical meteorological manifesto and studied every fableous fairytale ever after."

"There's a difference between understanding and doing," reminded her mother. The Snow Queen nodded to her husband. Clearly, they had discussed all of this. There were things Crystal needed to know. It was time.

The king looked back toward the throne room and waved his scepter over the ice. From the shiny surface bloomed a beautiful crystal rose. The queen gestured with her hand, and a breeze lifted the sparkling blossom into the air.

"Soon, my dear," began the queen, "you will blossom like this enchanted Winter Rose."

"And become the next Snow Queen," added her father.

The air was crisp and cold, but Crystal felt warm inside. Her parents loved her, they believed in her, and they were preparing her for her place in the world. All was right in their fairytale kingdom. How could they know that Jackie Frost and Northwind were right above, looking down on them, waiting to create a happily-never-after ending to their tale?

Jackie held the envelope. With her other hand, she pulled a long, thin straw out of her pocket. A pixie, seeing them, became alarmed. Who were these frost elves? What were they up to?

Jackie dipped the straw into the envelope of perilous purple powder. Northwind protected his face with his scarf. With a tap of her finger, Jackie scattered the devilish dust over the royal family. Glints of purple mingled with the snowflakes. Evil was in the air!

But just as the cold cloud descended, Crystal stepped backward into the throne room, escaping the dust entirely. Her parents rubbed their eyes. What was that? They blinked. They stiffened. They shook themselves. They peered out at their kingdom, but now it looked very different to them— very different indeed.

Jackie Frost quietly clapped her hands. Her plan was working!

Brooke was confused. What was this dust? Where had it come from?

Brooke stopped her parents in midstory and flipped backward in her fairytale book. In the last chapter, Ever After High had faced its greatest villain ever—the Evil Queen from Snow White's tale. Brooke looked at the picture of Snow White's daughter, Apple, gazing at the Evil Queen through the magic mirror.

Apple White was angry at the Evil Queen. She had an apple in her hand, and she hurled it at the mirror! The mirror shattered into a million pieces, each one of them as tiny as a mote of dust, each one of them magically unlucky.

"Oh," Brooke murmured. "The Snow King's shapeshifting servants Jackie Frost and Northwind stole that potent source of evil. And that cannot be good."

From far, far away, the Evil Queen laughed.

CHAPTER 4

Below Freezing

The palace pixies were tugging at Crystal's dress, trying to get her attention. They were chattering and tittering about, well, *something*, but they were too frightened to make any sense. The Snow King and Snow Queen sneezed at the exact same moment—and the shrieking pixies skittered away, alarmed.

Crystal hadn't noticed anything. She was admiring her beautiful ice rose. "Thank you for this promise rose, Mom and Dad," she said, smiling. "I won't let you down."

The Snow Queen frowned. She snatched the rose out of the air angrily. "You've already let me down with this ingratitude."

"You're acting like a spoiled brat," complained the Snow King, scowling.

"What are you saying?" Crystal was baffled. She had just told them how grateful she was. It was as if they hadn't heard what she said.

They hadn't. They saw everything through a haze of evil magic-mirror dust. Even now they thought she was thumbing her nose at them. They heard her say, "You are old and frostbitten. I could rule winter better with my eyes closed."

The king and queen stormed past their daughter. Snow whirled around them. They were furious!

"She gets this lack of respect from you! She acts too silly to rule!" raged the Snow Queen.

Crystal had never heard her parents argue before. Why were they being so mean to each other? Why were they so angry at her? She raced after them to find out.

The pixies were wringing their hands. They didn't know what to do. A blizzard was blowing up between the king and queen.

"Silly, huh?" the king fumed. "You must think I'm nothing but a snow goose. I should freeze-tag you right now so you cool down!"

"Oh, I'd like to see you try, snowman!" yelled the queen. She shook the rose in his face.

The king froze her. Solid. He had turned his wife into an ice sculpture.

The courtiers gasped. Crystal was beyond words. What was happening?

The king turned on them with a menacing look. "Who else wants to play freeze tag?"

In the background, Jackie and Northwind cackled with glee.

"Your Highness..." one of the braver elves began politely.

But the king experienced a very different reality. What he heard was one of his subjects mocking him, saying "Look at me! I'm the Snow King. This is what I sound like!" The king thought the elf was making insulting raspberry noises.

But he wasn't.

The Snow King's eyes narrowed as he studied the elf. "You should learn to be more sheepish," he said. He waved his scepter, and a blast of magic hit the elf, turning him into a snow sheep!

"Baa!" bleated what was once an elf.

Crystal turned her hockey stick back into a wand as fast as she could. She held it up in front of her defensively. "Dad," she ordered, "unfreeze Mom right now."

"I would, but she's giving me the cold shoulder." He cackled devilishly.

Crystal stomped her foot. "If this is a game, it's not funny anymore. What has gotten into you?"

"Playtime is over, Princess," announced the king. A glint of purple sparkled in his eyes. "Your mother was right about one thing—you are too childish to rule!"

Crystal didn't know what to do, but she knew she had to get away. She skated out of the throne room as fast as she could. The pixies hurried after her.

In her own room, she burst into tears. Her parents had never been so mean to her. The pixies patted her shoulder and made little noises of concern.

"What's wrong with wanting to have some fun?" asked Crystal. "I don't belong here anymore."

Through her tears, Crystal noticed a photo of herself and her Ever After High friends Ashlynn Ella and Briar Beauty. She missed them. A lot. Maybe it was time to pay them a visit and return to school.

"I know where they'll be warm to me," she told the pixies. "In a land not-so-far, far away."

From the tippy-top of a turret, Jackie Frost and Northwind watched as Crystal slipped out of the castle by herself. They saw her trudging through the snow, headed away from the top of the world. Northwind clapped his hands with delight. Jackie grinned. Her plan was working even better than she'd imagined!

CHAPTER 5

First Frost

Ever After High's castle still had not recovered from the Evil Queen's brief takeover. The stones were dirty and the windows were grimy. It just didn't gleam the way a fairytale castle should. This was most upsetting to Headmaster Grimm.

When the class bell rang, he called Faybelle Thorn into his office. Faybelle was destined to be the next Dark Fairy in the tale of Sleeping Beauty; she was perfectly happy with her fate and never missed a chance to get involved with trouble. She could barely contain her boredom while the headmaster scolded her about helping out the Evil Queen.

"I am fairy, fairy disappointed in you," said Headmaster Grimm. "Your involvement with the Evil Queen has left this school a vile mess."

Faybelle tossed her lush platinum mane. "Oh, come on. It's not that bad."

A crumbling ceiling tile clunked onto the headmaster's desk. Faybelle pursed her lips, trying to hide her amusement. She loved disarray and destruction. She lived for it, really.

The headmaster sighed. "Don't get me wrong. I'm delighted you are following your evil destiny. But you must be punished, so I'm charging you with cleaning duties until our school is restored to its former pristine glory."

Faybelle's face fell. "Clean up the whole school by myself? That'll take forever after!"

"Then I suggest you get started," answered the headmaster.

Grumbling, Faybelle left his office with a bucket and a mop. She fluttered her tiny iridescent wings—and nearly flew right into Daring Charming and Apple White. That was the last thing she needed! She avoided looking at the goody-goody couple as she passed.

But Daring and Apple were almost as unhappy as Faybelle. Something was the matter—and Blondie Lockes, Ever After High's hotshot reporter, had spotted the scoop. Such as it was. If only there were more interesting news to report!

She popped up between them, her microphone held out. "Blondie Lockes here, with another relationship rumor-cast. The whole school knows that Daring Charming's kiss was a total fairy-fail when he couldn't wake Apple White from her enchanted sleep—aka he's *not* her destined prince! *Awk*ward. Is this power couple about to power off?" She stuck her microphone in their faces. "Daring? Apple? Care to comment?"

Daring's handsome face reddened. "Not really."

"Uh, no," replied Apple.

Blondie looked dissatisfied, but what could she do? It was the only story she had.

Elsewhere in the school, students checked in on Blondie's always popular MirrorCast.

Ashlynn Ella, Cinderella's daughter, watched with concern. "Have you noticed, Briar," she said to her best friend, "Blondie's reporting lately has been not…"

"Not *just right*," completed Briar, using the familiar phrase from the story of Blondie's mother, Goldilocks. "Definitely."

The girls were too busy chatting to see their old friend slip through the front door of the high school. Crystal hid behind a pillar to surprise Ashlynn and Briar. With a flip of her wand, she created a cold gust of wind.

"Brrrr," shivered Briar. "Did you feel that?"

"It just got freezing in here," Ashlynn agreed.

Crystal waved her wand. It started to snow.

Ashlynn smiled, realizing what was going on. "Wait a spell…is that snow?"

"Impossible! It's summer," said Briar, still confused by the unexpected weather. "Unless…"

"She's here!" shouted both girls, delighted. But where was she?

"She must be around here somewhere," they said. The pair noticed the ice sculpture of a unicorn first, and in the next instant, their friend.

She grinned. "I thought I would melt in this heat! Ever After High really needs an air conditioner."

"Crystal!" exclaimed the girls.

"Ashlynn! Briar!"

They hugged one another and fell into a soft drift of newly fallen snow. Laughing, they made snow angels together.

"It's been too long! It's fableous to see you!" Ashlynn said with a smile.

Students were passing, waving at Crystal. She waved back happily.

"We're fairy glad to see you," said Briar. "But what are you doing here?"

Crystal paused for a moment. Should she tell them what was happening with her parents? Maybe not yet. She forced a casual smile. "Do I need an excuse to visit my best friends forever after?"

She waved her wand again, frosting a row of lockers.

"Of course not, Crystal," Briar answered. Still, she was troubled. She could tell her friend was hiding something.

"Now, how about we sparklize these dusty halls?" suggested Crystal, changing the subject. She let out a blast of glittering energy from her sparklizer, filling the air with shimmering crystals. It was just what everyone wanted on a hot, hot day. At least for a little bit.

CHAPTER 6

Snow Day

*H*eadmaster Grimm was hard at work in his office. Finally, he realized snow was covering his papers. He shook it off and continued writing with his feather pen. A crowd of students had collected outside his door. They were waiting for him to make an announcement, but he wasn't paying any attention to them.

"Come on, come on," urged Duchess Swan under her breath as more students gathered around.

The headmaster swept another inch of snow off his desk.

"Say it," Lizzie Hearts begged, shaking with anticipation. "You can do it. You can do it."

More students crowded close, craning their necks to see the headmaster. Was it going to happen? It had to!

At last the headmaster couldn't stand it. He couldn't

ignore the weather anymore. "All right, fine," he said, sighing. He grabbed the microphone. It was covered in icicles. He cleared his throat. The loudspeaker crackled. "Attention, students. Classes are dismissed for Ever After High's first ever *summer* snow day."

The students cheered. Whoops and hollers echoed through the hallways. Lockers slammed as kids grabbed their backpacks and headed outside to throw snowballs.

Uh-oh. A snowball flew through the open window and smacked the headmaster on the side of his face. Winter was here, all right. No question about it.

More students celebrated their day off from classes in the Castleteria. Melody Piper was at her turntable, filling the room with music. "No need to bundle up," she told them with a laugh, "'cause DJ Melody's got hot tunes to keep you nice and warm."

Hunter Huntsman was busy sawing long planks of wood into snowboards. He handed one to his buddy Sparrow Hood. "Consider yourself challenged to a shred-off," said Hunter.

He hopped on his board and zoomed across the snow-filled room. Sparrow followed him, shredding his guitar while he snowboarded. "*Oww!* You're on!" he sang.

Sparrow whooshed past Kitty Cheshire, who was poised behind an enormous pile of snowballs. "Meow!" she purred, and hurled a snowball at Raven Queen.

Raven held up her hand and stopped the snowball in midair with a stream of purple magic. The snowball floated at a standstill—for a moment. Raven grinned. Uh-oh. Kitty's ears folded back as she realized what was about to happen. The snowball headed backward—in *her* direction!

"Nice try, snow cat," cackled Raven. She twirled her finger, and five more snowballs floated into the air. They all flew right at Kitty. Just in time, Kitty ducked behind a drift.

In the middle of the room was a brand-new ice-skating rink. Justine Dancer, the daughter of the Twelfth Dancing Princess, was twirling like a skating pro. She spun round and round while the crowd cheered.

Duchess Swan pushed through to see what all the fuss was about. "Whoa, hold the MirrorPhone," she told everyone. "I'm the best ice dancer around here."

Justine laughed as she kicked her leg up in the air, executing a perfect triple axel. "Do your thing, Duchess. I haven't met a dance yet I couldn't master."

Duchess was focused. She glided onto the ice. She circled Justine with perfect elegance. The two girls locked eyes as they competed. The music blared. The crowd was riveted. What a snow day!

In the back of the Castleteria, Crystal sat with her friends, surveying the action. Girls recognized her, waved, and giggled. Boys smiled at her and blushed. In a school full of storybook stars, she was a real celebrity.

Briar sighed happily. "After the year we've had, a little winter break is snow awesome."

"But tell us why you really came," Ashlynn said at last.

CHAPTER 7

Wicked Cool News

Crystal frowned. How could she explain what she didn't really understand? At last she said, "It's my parents. They haven't been themselves lately. Especially my dad. He's been so...cold."

"Isn't that kind of his thing?" Briar asked.

"No!" exclaimed Crystal. "I mean, he's mean. It's like he's twisting everything to see only bad." She paused. It was so painful to think about how her father had changed. She didn't even want to tell her friends what he'd done to her mother. "And let's just say my mom is a total ice queen all of a sudden. Life is snow unfair. I feel like I've been cursed."

Ashlynn nodded. "Maybe it *is* a curse."

"It happens," agreed Briar.

"You think I'm really cursed?" Crystal wondered aloud. She hadn't thought about that possibility.

"Your parents," said both her friends together.

Hunter and Sparrow zoomed past on their snowboards, but Crystal ignored them.

"As I was saying"—Ashlynn continued her thought—"nobody knows more about evil curses than Madam Baba Yaga. I bet she can help."

That was a great idea, Crystal realized. Her old teacher was a witch—a powerful witch and an expert on potions, spells, and curses of all kinds. "I knew my old BFFAs would make me feel better. Let's go see her."

Across the Castleteria, students' phones pinged with a mirror update. Blondie Lockes had a report on the snow day—but she didn't seem very eager. In fact, she seemed kind of bored. "Hello, everyone. Time for a weird weather report. Ever After High is like one big snow globe. But why? What's the snow scoop? Is the Evil Queen on the loose? Is it snow global warming? We may never know." Blondie stifled a yawn.

Cerise Hood poked into the frame. "Sure we do. Crystal Winter is visiting."

"Ever heard of suspense?" hissed Blondie. "Breaking news! The cause of this summer snow is the arrival of the Princess of Snow herself, Crystal Winter. Is she really the diva the tabloids say she is?"

The camera zoomed in on Crystal, who waved politely. "Hi, Blondie! I love your show!"

Blondie frowned. She couldn't figure out how to spin this news to make it exciting. "But is *everyone* thrilled with the chills Crystal has caused?" she asked, her voice low and ominous. Blondie stuck her microphone toward a few startled faces. If there wasn't any real news, she was going to make some up.

But it wasn't working.

"Crystal is cool!" enthused Duchess Swan.

"Wicked cool," Raven Queen agreed.

"I'm a big fan," Dexter Charming volunteered.

"She's the bee's knees," said Sparrow.

Foiled again. "Okay, cut." Blondie sighed. "This isn't news—it's fluff. Blondie Lockes signing off."

Cerise Hood had been watching her friend the whole time, and she was worried. When Blondie had stowed away her reporting gear, Cerise went over to join her. "This just in: Blondie Lockes needs to chill out. Everything just right, Blondie?"

"Spellebrity gossip and weather reports are so last chapter. I need a real news story. Something dangerous and hexciting. The kind of story that wins reporters a Princess and the Peabody Award."

Blondie sighed, daydreaming about stepping forward and thanking her family and her friends for supporting her journalistic accomplishments. How would it ever happen if *nothing* ever happened at Ever After High?

CHAPTER 8

Curses and Cocoa

*F*ar away from the snow-day festivities, Daring was sitting by himself in the hallway. He was upset.

Rosabella Beauty was skating by. She skidded to a stop when she saw him. "Daring Charming with a big frown on his face? What's going on?"

"I'm just so confused about what I'm supposed to do now that I'm not Apple's Prince Charming," he confessed.

Rosabella sat down beside him. She smoothed her gold skirt thoughtfully. She wanted to help Daring, even though there were some hard things she needed to tell him. But how? "Have you ever considered that you're not the prince of Apple's destiny because you haven't earned it yet?"

Daring blinked, confused. What was Rosabella saying? "*Earn* it?"

"Snow White's Prince Charming was bold, heroic...and selfless. Maybe it would help if you thought about helping somebody. You know, somebody who wasn't...*you*."

But Daring hadn't heard Rosabella. He was gazing at his own handsome reflection in the ice. He smoothed back his hair to get a better look at his profile. He realized Rosabella was staring at him.

"Oh, I'm sorry," Daring apologized. "I got distracted. What were you talking about? Something about me, right?"

Rosabella shook her head. Well, she'd tried.

Meanwhile, Ashlynn, Briar, and Crystal were stepping into Baba Yaga's office. The books and the desks were covered in snow. Baba Yaga was hovering in front of a steaming cauldron, tossing in bits of this and bundles of that. The old witch was stirring up a magic potion.

"Madam Baba Yaga," Ashlynn interrupted as politely as she could. "You know a lot about curses, right?"

"What?" The witch whirled around, suddenly defensive. "Who said anything about a curse? No curses here. You can't prove anything. Who sent you?"

"No," Briar reassured her. "It's Crystal's dad, the Snow King. We think he might be cursed."

The witch nodded as she sprinkled a fine dust over the surface of the bubbling liquid.

"Madam Baba Yaga, can you help?" begged Crystal.

"No promises, child," Baba Yaga wheezed. "It depends

on the kind of curse. Bring your father to me and I'll see what I can do."

Baba Yaga tossed a handful of glowing dragon's teeth into her potion—and it exploded. *Boom!* A cloud of thick smoke filled the room. When it had cleared, a tray with four big mugs of hot cocoa with tiny marshmallows appeared. She picked up the tray and offered each girl a steaming mug.

"Yummy!" Baba Yaga smacked her lips. "Hot cocoa made with fresh pig's breath!"

The girls hesitated, their mugs at their lips. Crystal set hers down on a desk. "So we just have to figure out how to get my dad to come to Ever After High…"

Briar's eyes lit up. "I've got an idea!"

And all they needed to do was send an invitation!

CHAPTER 9

Storm Clouds

The Snow King slumped on his throne. He was in a foul mood. His wife was still frozen solid, and the king had thrown his robe over her outstretched arm as if she were a coatrack.

"Where is my snow-flakey daughter?" he demanded.

A frost elf stepped forward timidly. "I believe she went to visit her old friends. She sent you this invitation." He opened a letter and began reading. "'You are cordially invited to attend the Ever After High Royal Career Day.'"

The king scowled as he listened, clearly displeased. What he heard the elf saying, through the aura of the curse, was "Your job is so easy a dim-witted bridge troll with an ice tray could do it as well as you."

"What did she say to me?" he shouted, furious.

The frost elf was baffled. Why was the Snow King so upset? But before he could say anything else, the king raised his scepter—and turned the elf into a penguin! The king strode across the throne room, fuming. Terrified elves and panicked pixies scattered as fast as they could.

"I'll teach them to mock my royal position," he fumed. "Make ready my sleigh! I'm going to Ever After High!"

Jackie Frost and Northwind stepped forward. "We'll do it, Your Winterness," Jackie said eagerly.

The king nodded, grumbled, and stomped out of the throne room.

Northwind grabbed Jackie. "I thought you didn't want to take orders anymore," he whispered.

"Keep it down, slush brain," Jackie said under her breath. "The king has clearly flipped his crown. Just as we planned. And his daughter has flown the coop. But if he's going to where Crystal is, we'll follow him—and, let's just say, *close the chapter* on her story."

"Oh, I get it!" Northwind nodded. He winked at Jackie. "It'll be *The End* for Crystal Winter."

Jackie groaned. She grabbed her sidekick by the goggles and yanked him after her. They had a sleigh to get ready.

CHAPTER 10

Breaking the Ice

Parents crowded into the snowy Ever After High auditorium for Career Day. Apple White entered with her beautiful mother, Snow White. Raven pushed a large magic mirror down the aisle so her mother, the Evil Queen, could participate. The Billy Goats Gruff were with their son Billy, and the Cheshire Cat was with Kitty.

The Evil Queen leered menacingly from her mirror. "Boo!" she shouted—and the Billy Goats leaped into the air.

From the stage, Briar, Ashlynn, and Crystal anxiously watched the guests arriving. Would the Snow King show up? If he did, Baba Yaga was ready to check for curses.

"Thanks for making Career Day happen, everyone," Crystal told her friends. "This is a great trap!"

Baba Yaga grinned. "I am always happy to arrange school functions for the purposes of deception."

"So many parents came to talk," Ashlynn noted thoughtfully. "Your dad will never suspect we're trying to pull the crown over his eyes."

"Are you sure he'll fall for it?" asked Briar.

Crystal scanned the room. "Oh, he'll be here," she said. "My dad won't be able to resist. He may be wicked cold, but he's full of hot air."

"Don't worry, Crystal," said Ashlynn reassuringly. "We'll get to the bottom of this." *Poor Crystal,* she thought.

Far from the festivities, up on the top of a turret, Faybelle was hard at work scrubbing away evil grime. She was strapped into a harness and grumbling as she ran her washer up and down over the dingy tiles. She squinted as she saw a sleigh pulled by polar bears approaching the castle. It pulled up right in front!

"You there! You there, boy!" said the Snow King imperiously to Daring, who was working on a snow sculpture. "Come here. My bears need to be watered, fed, and stabled."

"That's not really *my* job," said Daring.

The Snow King's face turned red. This petulant boy was ignoring him! "Boy, I said, *come here*!"

"Can't you see I'm busy?" Daring answered without moving. "I'm trying to cheer myself up with a 'snow me.'"

But the Snow King was not impressed with Daring's snowy replica of himself. He raised his scepter. "I'll give you one more chance, boy. Or do I have to spell it out for you?"

Daring ignored the Snow King and put his mirror in the hand of the sculpture. Perfect! "There we go!" he said, pleased with himself. Then he realized the Snow King was staring at him. "Oh, you're still there?"

"You beastly young man," the Snow King hissed through gritted teeth. "You will regret this forever after!"

He sent a blast of icy magic right at Daring. It swirled around the prince—and disappeared inside him. Daring rubbed his head. He felt a little funny, a little different, a little off. What was it? He shrugged. He looked at his sculpture again. It needed one more thing. Ah! A crown—that was it. He took the one off his own head and put it on his snow double. What he didn't notice was the little tuft of white fur sprouting on the back of his neck.

One of the sleigh bears twitched his nose. He smelled something—another animal. But where was it?

CHAPTER 11

Chilled to the Bone

The Snow King burst through the front door of Ever After High in a huff. Luckily, the girls were waiting for him.

"Welcome, Your Majesty, to our Career Day spellebration," Briar greeted him.

Ashlynn smiled sweetly. "So nice to see you again, Your Highness."

The Snow King ignored them, staring instead at the snow-covered hall. "Oh, I get it," he sneered. "You filled the school with snow to show me you think you can do my job better than I can."

"Uh…no…we just thought," Briar stammered, "that it would make you feel at home?"

Baba Yaga floated over to the Snow King, her hand held

out, welcoming him. Before he could do anything, she was examining his palm for hexes. "Tell me," she asked him, "have you recently angered or incurred the wrath of some kind of troll or dark sorcerer?"

Baba Yaga sniffed the Snow King's palm. She put her ear to his chest to listen to the beating of his heart.

The king was too surprised to react at first. "Madam, what are you—"

"Say *aaah*!" commanded Baba Yaga.

But the Snow King yanked his hand away from her. "Take those bony, callused hands off me, you witch."

He tapped his scepter, and a cold blast of wind encased Baba Yaga in snow. He marched past the girls toward the auditorium.

"Um, royally rude," gulped Briar.

"Crystal's right," Ashlynn agreed. "That's not the Snow King I know."

Baba Yaga shook off her covering of snow. "He'd better be cursed, or he will be when I'm done with him. Let's get to work!"

Outdoors, two of the polar bears had transformed—back into Jackie and Northwind.

"Bear with it!" joked Northwind.

Jackie grimaced. "You say that joke every time you take bear form."

"It's that funny. So, what's next?"

"What's next is we make sure the Snow King freezes out Crystal—his only heiress to the throne."

Northwind nodded, following Jackie into the school.

In the auditorium, the Cheshire Cat was finishing her speech to the audience. "Then you turn invisible, leaving only your grin!"

"Hooray!" cheered Kitty. "Wow!"

The Cheshire Cat vanished—save for her mysterious smile. Kitty applauded wildly, but the rest of the audience wasn't exactly sure how this could help them after they graduated. There were a few polite claps and some muffled laughter.

Headmaster Grimm took the stage next. "Thank you, Mrs. Cheshire, for that very useful presentation in the etiquette of invisibility." He took a sip of coffee from the cup in his hand and prepared to introduce the next presenter.

The Snow King was standing backstage, waiting to go on. Ashlynn and Briar were trying to distract him while Baba Yaga sneaked up from behind and examined his ears. She peered over his shoulder at his beard, and he swatted her hand away as if it were a fly.

"And now please give a warm welcome to the Snow King!" announced the headmaster.

The Snow King strutted onto the stage and held up his hand. "No, no applause. There is nothing fun about winter. It's dark and cold and unforgiving. Like me. And I control it all. Does that chill you to the bone? I could turn you into a waddle of penguins with a flick of my wrist. Haha!" he cackled maliciously.

Students cowered in their seats. The Snow King waved

his scepter. Parents smiled nervously. A few kids looked at Crystal inquisitively. *What's going on?* But she could only shrug. If only she knew!

Baba Yaga crept up behind the Snow King again. Her examination was almost over. "Yep, definitely cursed," she muttered.

"You wretched creature," exclaimed the Snow King, whirling around.

He fired his scepter. The crowd gasped and murmured. The king was angry now. Really, really angry. What no one knew was that when he looked out at the audience, he saw eyes glowing with rage and heard the evil mutterings of people out to get him.

"Such insolence!" screamed the Snow King. "You people don't even deserve to be penguins!"

He was holding his scepter aloft, and it glowed purple with evil magic. "I'll put all of you on ice!" he warned.

But just as he was about to unleash his fury, a bolt of ice magic froze his arm in place. It was Crystal! "That's enough, Dad," she said as calmly as she could. "Stop. We are trying to help. Dad, please, you are not seeing things clearly."

With his other hand, her father zapped her. Crystal staggered backward, the power in her wand drained.

"Oh, I am seeing you clearly," bellowed her father. "Betrayer, daughter, you will never sit on my throne. No ice powers forever after! You are disempowered!"

The Snow King snatched Crystal's wand from her trembling hand. Tears filled her eyes, but her father only laughed.

He slammed his scepter down, unleashing a blizzard of ice magic. The wind blew. The auditorium darkened. Swirling snow filled the air.

"I expect you home by curfew!" the Snow King commanded Crystal before storming out of the castle.

He swept past Jackie Frost and Northwind, unable to see them through the whiteness of the blizzard.

Jackie was delighted. "And that, dear brother, is what we call 'the Frost twins one step closer to ruling winter.'"

Daring, arriving late to the auditorium, couldn't figure out what was going on. "Man, who invited that guy?" he wondered. He scratched his itchy hand and noticed a tiny patch of white fur growing near his wrist.

Blondie Lockes staggered through the wind to the front of the auditorium. She was determined to report on the blizzard. Now, *this* was a weather report. "The snowstorm of the century is one massive Snow King tantrum! I think I just found my big story. Better make some notes."

But Crystal was despondent. How could her father be so cruel? "I had chosen to follow my destiny to be the next Snow Queen, but my future just got blown away."

CHAPTER 12

Whiteout

The blizzard gusted outside the castle, but Blondie braved the whirling whiteness to make her Mirror-Cast. With one gloved hand, she gripped the balcony railing so she wouldn't be blown away, and with the other, she clutched her microphone.

"Blondie Lockes reporting live outside Ever After High, where the weather is just *so* not right!"

Students and their parents leaving the auditorium were swept this way and that way by the wild winter winds. Professor Rumpelstiltskin slammed into an ice-covered window just below the balcony.

"And if the storm outside isn't bad enough," said Blondie, "it's twice as bad inside!"

Kids staggered down the hallways, trying not to get lost in

the whiteout. The wind extinguished their lanterns. They could barely make out the gray shadows of their friends. Humphrey Dumpty and Jillian Beanstalk clutched each other, shivering. They bumped into Hopper Croakington II, son of the Frog Prince, whose tongue was glued to his locker by the cold! They tried to pull him free and fell over backward into a snowbank.

The staircase had become a steep ski slope. Apple was carefully scaling it with the help of the Billy Goats—and ice-climbing gear. "Got...to get...to class," she panted.

"If the Snow King wanted to blast us away with his blizzard powers," Blondie reported, "mission accomplished!"

Jackie Frost and Northwind watched Blondie's Mirror-Cast with delight.

"Wow! Your whole curse-the-king plan is really working!" Northwind praised his sister. "He's on an evil roll!"

"I know! He's made his queen into an ice sculpture, changed half his servants into penguins, and taken away his daughter's wand of power! He's close to a snow blowout!" Jackie surveyed the frozen picture before her, smirking. "Then we will rule all of winter. We just have to keep an eye on the lazy princess, and then winter will be ours!"

After the freezing fiasco in the auditorium, Crystal fled to her friends' dorm room in despair. They tried to comfort her—but it was no use.

"What-ever-after are we going to do about this weather?" Ashlynn wondered aloud.

"I'm sorry," Crystal said, weeping. "But without my wand there's nothing I can do."

Briar nodded. "Her powers are totally in the deep freeze."

Raven and her pet dragon, Nevermore, joined them. "Here comes the fire department," she announced. She pointed Nevermore toward the hearth, where she breathed out a ball of flames. The poor dragon looked exhausted. She'd been working overtime to keep the castle's fireplaces lit. The girls warmed their hands and thanked Raven and Nevermore, who wearily headed out to continue trying to beat back the cold.

Blondie wanted to interview Crystal to get the scoop on the snow story. "Question: Your dad breezed out so fast on Career Day. Has he always been so stormy?"

"No!" protested Crystal. "He used to be the polar opposite!" She pulled out her phone and began showing Blondie photos from sunnier times. "We know he's been cursed," she continued. "I wish Baba Yaga had gotten more time to examine him."

"Wish," repeated Ashlynn. "That gives me an idea!"

Maybe it was the fire, or maybe Ashlynn's bright idea, but the girls suddenly weren't feeling so cold anymore!

CHAPTER 13

Unbearably Selfish

The blizzard was not making it any easier for Faybelle to finish up her castle-cleaning project. "Headmaster Grimm set me up for a royal fairy-fail," she grumbled. The wind blew her back and forth, her hands were icy, and the water in her bucket kept freezing. "It'll take forever after to clean this castle myself. There has to be a way to get it done without actually working."

She pulled out her MirrorPhone and began scrolling through online ads. Spells? Potions? Enchantments? What was she looking for? Then she saw it. Her eyes sparkled. "'Call 1-900-Fairy-Mob. The Fairy Mobfather makes problems disappear!'" Maybe she could get this done after all—without turning into an arctic animal.

On the grounds of the castle, Daring barely noticed the wild weather. He was too busy creating another snow sculpture of himself. Rosabella shook her head sadly.

"How're you doing, Daring?" she asked him. "Thought any more about our chat? You know, things you need to work on?"

"Oh yes!" he answered eagerly. "And as soon as my new mirror arrives, I am going to take a good, hard look at myself."

Rosabella shook her head. That wasn't what she'd had in mind. But before she could say anything else, a snow goose arrived—with a delivery for Daring.

"Here it comes now," he said, pleased.

"Incoming!" honked the goose. He crash-landed in a snowbank.

"Disaster!" shouted Daring. "What do I do? Ah! Of course! Daring Charming to the rescue!"

Rosabella was stunned. Maybe Daring was learning how to really be a prince after all. "My hero," she whispered to herself hopefully. She watched him race over to the half-buried goose and begin digging. But he wasn't helping the exhausted bird—he was concerned only with his package.

"The mirror is safe! Everyone can relax." Daring sighed happily.

The goose tried to honk but merely spluttered out a beakful of snow. Rosabella pulled him to his feet and helped him out of the snowbank. "Are you all right?" she asked the bird. When he had recovered, she turned on the prince. "Daring, this is exactly what I'm talking about. You're supposed to be a hero. Helping. Not just looking down your nose at…"

A purple miasma was swirling around Daring's head. Something was happening to him. It wasn't part of the blizzard; it was some other kind of magic. The cloud clustered and settled on Daring's nose, and when it cleared, the prince had been transformed. Where his nose had been was now a polar bear's giant black snout! Rosabella was speechless.

But Daring seemed to have no idea what had happened to him. He tucked the mirror under his arm and marched back into the high school, as sure of his good looks as ever.

Students stared and whispered to one another.

Raven gawked. "I can't believe it!"

"It's ginormous!" Cedar Wood exclaimed.

"I know!" Daring grinned, overhearing her. "It's the biggest mirror I could order."

CHAPTER 14

A Speck of Evil

Ashlynn told her friends her idea to stop the Snow King, and they rushed to Baba Yaga to see if she had any advice for them. Along the way, they grabbed some of their friends who might be helpful. They found the witch brewing up another potion in the auditorium, tossing bundles of herbs and gooey bits of this and that into her cauldron.

"So," Ashlynn explained, "Crystal was wishing that we could turn back the clock to when the Snow King stood right here on the stage. And I realized that there is a way. But we need everyone here to help, especially Farrah."

Farrah Goodfairy was the daughter of the Fairy Godmother and one of the most caring students at Ever After High. Her blue eyes sparkled with eagerness to lend a hand to her friends.

Baba Yaga considered Ashlynn's plan. It made sense to her. "Yes, yes, a magical reenactment." She directed Hopper Croakington to stand where the Snow King had been. She asked Farrah if she had brought her wand.

Farrah smiled proudly. "A good fairy-godmother-in-training always comes prepared." She waved her wand, wafting glittering trails of magic around the auditorium. Wherever her enchanted glimmer dust landed, the memory of Career Day reappeared—the posters on the wall, the decorations, the sparkling winter wonderland before the snarling blizzard. At last Farrah spun her wand around Hopper—turning him into an exact replica of the Snow King!

"Hey, look!" Hopper laughed, strutting across the stage and glowering.

"Nice fairy glamour," complimented Crystal.

"Wow, it looks like we're right back at Career Day," Ashlynn agreed. This was even better than she'd imagined.

"Why, thank you!" Farrah blushed. "I've been practicing."

Now their job was to look for clues to the curse. Where could the evil be hiding?

"What does evil even look like?" Briar wondered.

The girls searched backstage and under the seats and behind the curtain. They peered under the podium and they studied the rafters. Farrah kept her wand raised, concentrating on the enchantment.

"How long can you maintain this illusion?" asked Blondie.

"My transformations last until twelve. Midnight or noon. Whichever comes first."

Crystal examined Hopper-turned-into-the-Snow-King. He looked just like her father; still, something told her he was different, just a little bit different from the sweet father she had always known. What was it? Not his hair or his clothes or his face. *Wait a minute!* She peered into his eyes. A tiny speck of purple glinted in one of his pupils.

"Baba Yaga!" she called. "Quick! Here!"

Baba Yaga pulled out an enormous jeweler's magnifying glass from her pocket. She held it up to Hopper's face. A tiny shard from a mirror was embedded in the Snow King's eye—and in that mirror was reflected the face of the Evil Queen.

Baba Yaga shuddered. "That's the tiniest granule of pure evil I have ever seen. It's made from a shard of the Evil Queen's magic mirror."

How could this have happened? That was the question.

The girls clustered around Baba Yaga as she brought out her crystal ball. It glowed brightly—and an image formed within it. The crystal ball showed Crystal on the balcony with her parents.

"Someone close to the Snow King is behind this," noted Baba Yaga.

Unfortunately, the picture was vague and shifting, and it was hard to see exactly what was happening. But they could all see the purple flickers of evil falling through the snow—and landing in the Snow King's eye. They watched as the king's contented smile turned into a hateful scowl.

"The evil speck cursed him to only see bad in the world," Baba Yaga explained. "It seems your mother was also infected."

Baba Yaga wrapped an arm around Crystal. She knew this news was hard. She gave her a reassuring squeeze.

Farrah dropped her wand, and the illusion of Career Day vanished. The room grew dark and cold again. "Phew!" exhaled Farrah, exhausted.

Hopper was happy to be himself again.

But Crystal was more upset than ever, thinking of what was happening to her family. "My poor parents. We have to help them—or this wicked winter will last forever after."

CHAPTER 15

Arctic Blast

The Snow King returned to his kingdom and his castle in a foul mood. The ice sculpture of the queen still sparkled in the throne room. The king brooded on his throne. Trembling, a frightened frost elf polished the king's boots.

"Hurry up, servant," ordered the king. "I want my boots to shine as much as my queen does."

"Yes, Your Majesty! All done!"

But that wasn't what the king heard. Instead, he heard the frost elf insult him, saying, "You're a big dumb icicle with a snow cone for a brain."

"The insubordination around here!" bellowed the king, more furious than ever. He zapped the elf with his scepter and turned him into a baby harp seal. The poor elf-turned-seal flopped and barked across the ice-covered room.

"Everyone is plotting against me!" fumed the cursed Snow King to his frozen wife. "Even our own daughter! Well, let them try!"

* * *

At Ever After High, the blizzard blew harder than before. Snow drifted. Students shivered. Would it ever be warm again? Only Jackie and Northwind were happy.

Northwind happily sledded down a huge snowbank. "Wow, the king really went full arctic blast on this school."

"That's what we *want*," Jackie emphasized. "The king is out of control and driving away everyone who used to adore him. Soon he'll be ice-olated, and we can take him down, just us two."

Northwind was barely listening to Jackie. He was wiggling through the snow. "Look, I'm a snow worm!" he laughed.

"You have the brain of a snow worm," muttered Jackie.

What she didn't know was that Crystal and her friends were hard at work with Baba Yaga to save the Snow King and remove the shard of mirror from his eye. They were in the witch's office surrounded by jars containing everything from webbed wings to crawling spiders.

Briar was concerned. "So there's no magical eyewash to remove the evil glass from the Snow King's eye?"

Baba Yaga considered the idea. "Intriguing. Come to think of it, there might be a countercurse in the ancient scroll of *Deep Magic*. But the last known copy was in the Library of Elders."

"Wasn't that, like, totally destroyed a thousand years ago by the giants of Beanstalk High after we beat them at book-ball?" Ashlynn remembered.

"Well, yes," said Crystal thoughtfully. "But anything that has been decimated can be re-created. At least temporarily. Right, Farrah? Can you do one more glamour spell? Pretty please? It's a big one."

"I like a challenge!" Farrah said. "Let's conjure up some answers. To the library! Or the place where it was!"

Baba Yaga poured a dark brown liquid from her cauldron into a row of mugs. "Cocoa, anyone?"

Briar glanced at the jars of spiders behind her. "Sorry, Madam Baba Yaga. Gotta go!"

They had no time to lose if they were going to save the Snow King!

CHAPTER 16

The Ice Beast

Rosabella was worried about Daring. She went up to his dorm room and knocked on his door. "Daring, I really need to see you," she called.

"Rosabella?" he answered, his voice strangely gruff. "There's nothing new or unusual going on with me. Hahaha!" He didn't invite her in.

"Open the door," she told him. But he didn't. She pushed against the door, but something was holding it shut—a large, white paw. Rosabella pushed harder, and all of a sudden the door flew open. Daring was on his bed, under the covers, his face buried in a book.

"What are you doing?" Rosabella asked suspiciously.

"Catching up on homework," mumbled Daring. "Oops,

my quill fell under the bed." He rolled between the mattress and the wall and disappeared under his bed. When he reappeared, he was wrapped even tighter in his comforter.

"Brrr," he said. "Still so cold."

"Drop the comforter, Daring," Rosabella ordered. "I can see the fur on your toes."

"Those are just my new fuzzy slippers," he protested.

"Let me see you." She yanked off the comforter and gasped. Daring was completely transformed into an ice beast.

"Don't look at me," he begged. "I'm hideous."

Rosabella shrugged. "No. You're still you."

"I don't know who I am anymore," he said, sobbing. "Without my looks, I'm nothing. Nothing."

"It's not the end of the world," said Rosabella gently. "I know you want to be a prince, but maybe you're a beast."

"No one *wants* to be a *beast!*" Daring cried.

"Um, my *dad* is a beast," Rosabella reminded him.

Daring's cries turned into coughs, and his coughing turned into choking—and a large, white fuzz ball emerged from his mouth. Daring stared at it.

"It's a hair ball," explained Rosabella.

Daring was horrified. "Prince Charming does. Not. Get. *Hair balls!*"

"You put all your focus on the outside," said Rosabella, "instead of what's on the inside. Maybe all this fur has something to do with your destiny."

"It's okay." Daring sighed, trying to pull himself together.

"I'm still handsome, just in a furry kind of way." He opened the door of his room bravely. "I have nothing to hide."

"You sure you want to do that?" Rosabella asked as Daring headed down the hallway. She trailed after him nervously.

"What's new, girls?" said Daring the Beast, strutting up to a crew of students standing around their ice-covered lockers.

They gasped. They screamed. They tittered.

"It's me—Daring," he said. "I've still got it, right?"

Madeline Hatter shook her head. "That's a face only a mama bandersnatch could love."

"Daring, what happened to you?" Apple exclaimed a she came down the hall. "You're a beast!"

Daring was crushed. "No," he protested. "It's a phase."

No one knew what to say.

"You think I'm a joke, don't you?" he said, upset. "Don't judge me!" He scurried down the hallway, bawling huge ice-beast tears that froze in midair. The Snow King's curse was causing trouble for everyone.

CHAPTER 17

Left Out in the Cold

Faybelle Thorne was scrubbing another tower. She was covered in ice. She was grumbling. She didn't see the three mob fairies coming until they were up close.

"We were sent by the Fairy Mobfather," the biggest one said out of the corner of his mouth. "Maybe you need a little... *'sumpin sumpin'* ... ya know?"

"Yes!" exclaimed Faybelle. *What a relief!* "You got my message. Fableous. Do you do castle restoration?"

"You betcha," another of the mobsters said, chuckling. "No mess too big!"

"Then get cracking!" said Faybelle. "I've been working my wings off all day."

The head mobster took a look at the grime-covered castle. "Sure ya have, doll."

"Just so we have an understanding," added the third mobster. "We provide valuable services, right? We solve your problem, you owe us."

Faybelle nodded. She just wanted to get inside and get warm! "Deal! What-ever-after. I need a breather."

Faybelle wasn't even inside before the mob fairies were done. The castle gleamed in the snow. There wasn't a speck of dirt anywhere. It was glorious. Faybelle was stunned.

"Okay, kid," said the head mobster. "Take a look."

"You're done?" Faybelle couldn't believe it.

"Yeah, yeah," apologized the third mobster. "Sorry about the wait."

"Fairy, fairy impressive," enthused Faybelle.

"Thanks, doll." The mobster grinned and handed her a slip of paper. "Here's your bill."

Faybelle read it. She read it again. It couldn't be true! "Two hundred years of service! That's an ever after long time!"

The mob fairy shrugged. "We give you our time, you give us yours. That was our agreement. You nodded." He looked to his fellow mobsters. "She nodded, right?"

"Did I?" Faybelle gulped. "So what kind of service would I be doing for the next two hundred years?"

"A little bit of this. A little bit of that. Mostly hard labor."

"She's not gonna be a problem, is she?" whispered one of the mobsters to the other.

Faybelle was terrified. "There's got to be another way!"

But the mobsters didn't think so.

CHAPTER 18

Library Illusion

*C*rystal and her friends hurried through windy corridors toward the site of the long-lost library. Maybe there they would find the cure for the curse. They wound their way down a twisting staircase until they came to an enormous door with human-looking arms encircling it.

"The Library of Elders," announced Briar, awestruck.

Ashlynn tried to turn the door handle. It was locked. She sighed. "We can't catch a break."

"I've got this," said Blondie Lockes. "Locks are my thing. It's even in my name!"

She began picking the lock expertly. In a matter of minutes the doors flung open, revealing nothing beyond them but empty sky—and a dizzying drop to the ground. One step meant certain death.

Farrah rolled up the sparkly sleeves of her gown and got her wand ready. This was a big job, but she could do it. "One conjured library, coming right up!" She pointed her wand at the empty space. Sparkling energy swirled in the sky. "Look beyond the library door, and what was there before, *restore*!"

She shut her eyes tight, concentrating on the spell, and the olden room slowly materialized. Row upon dusty row of ancient books. Paneled walls. A marble floor. A ticking grandfather clock. Even the cobwebs.

Briar Beauty had just one concern. "Farrah, I hope your Goodfairy magic can hold our weight."

"Spelltacular!" Crystal said. But she was worried. Was Farrah up for this?

"I need to stay here to hold the spell," said Farrah, her eyes still shut. "You'd better hurry." Whatever she was doing, it was hard.

The girls knew their time was limited; they had until noon to find the ancient scroll of *Deep Magic*. If they didn't get back to Farrah before then, the conjured library would disappear and they would fall to their doom. They stepped onto the marble floor. It felt solid beneath their feet—for now.

"Over here," called Blondie, who was already exploring the narrow aisles of books.

The girls sped over to her. She was standing at a dead end, but she'd discovered a locked secret passage. There had to be a switch of some kind to open it, and the girls began a mad hunt to find it. They tugged on the nose of a nearby statue.

They pulled different books off the shelves. Blondie found the switch hidden beneath the globe—and the vault opened.

It was filled with dusty scrolls. Which one was *Deep Magic*? They didn't have time to check them all.

"*The Lazy Mud Prince,*" read Briar. "Glad he doesn't go to Ever After High."

Ashlynn picked up a scroll. "*The Slippery Slippers.* I don't think I'd want a pair of those."

Crystal stopped in her tracks. Across the vault, a scroll was unrolling all by itself—as if it had heard the girls talking about what they were looking for. "That must be the scroll of *Deep Magic*!"

The girls gathered around it. Blondie filmed it with her MirrorPhone.

"This explains how the Evil Queen's mirror was made," said Briar. "*Magic mirror glass is forged by goblins out of molten-hot evil pixie dust.*"

"*Exposure to particles of magic mirror glass,*" Ashlynn continued, "*can cause Kindness Blindness.* That sounds like what has happened to your parents."

"But does it talk about a cure?" asked Crystal, looking over the scroll herself.

As if in answer to her words, four roses magically appeared on the parchment.

"Aha!" exclaimed Crystal. "*Only the bouquet of the four Royal Roses of the Seasons has the power to undo the Kindness Blindness curse.* An aromatherapy cure!"

"Talk about a strong perfume," said Briar.

"These aren't just any roses," Crystal explained. "Each is one of a kind, and there's one for each season. They're enchanted." She studied the scroll again. There was some kind of riddle appearing under the picture of the four roses. *"Spring's Rose stands out, all alone. Summer's Rose wears a disguise. The Rose of Fall hides in the crowd. The Rose of Winter's found inside."*

"So we need to make a superpowered bouquet," Ashlynn decided. "Where are the roses?"

"They're royal property. Each one is at a different fairytale castle."

Blondie grinned excitedly. "You know what this means? Road trip!"

"But what castles are they at?" Crystal worried. "Ever After has so many."

The scroll was showing a series of different images. Blondie tried to capture each one with her camera.

"That's Beauty and the Beast's castle," Blondie realized. "Rosabella's palace."

"Look!" pointed Ashlynn. "My castle, too! And, Briar, that's your place."

Another castle was shimmering into view as the clock began to chime. It was just seconds from noon! There was no time left.

"Hurry!" Farrah called from far away. "I can't make this magic much longer."

Ashlynn peered at the scroll, but the magic was already fading. They hadn't seen the last castle!

Bong! Bong! Bong! The grandfather clock was tolling down the seconds. In an instant the library would disappear.

"Three out of four ain't bad," said Blondie. The vault began to shake. Books were falling all around them. Shelves were disappearing. The floor was breaking apart. "We gotta get outta here. Now!"

The girls raced as fast as they could toward the door. *Bong! Bong! Bong!*

"We've lost track of time," moaned Farrah. She was trying with all her might to maintain the magic.

"Farrah, stay strong," begged Blondie when she reached her friend's side.

"*Aaargh!* I can't beat the clock!" the fairy cried.

Ashlynn leaped through thin air toward Farrah. She landed with a thud on the solid floor. The other girls followed in the nick of time—all except Crystal. "Crystal, jump!" Ashlynn urged her friend.

But Crystal was frozen with terror. "My pixies always help me when I'm in trouble."

"Your pixies aren't here," answered Ashlynn.

"Jump!" screamed Blondie.

Crystal shut her eyes and leaped into the air just as the final bit of marble floor vanished beneath her feet. She flew through the air, reached toward her friends—and was just able to grip the edge of the door with her fingers. She was dangling above the terrible drop.

"Hold on!" begged Ashlynn as the girls struggled to pull their friend to safety.

The doors slammed shut. They'd made it.

Crystal was exhilarated. She'd done it! "Farrah, you are amazing! That was close!"

It certainly was! The girls hugged one another, trembling and laughing at the same time.

CHAPTER 19

Curse Curing

Blondie began reporting on the incident as soon as she had caught her breath. "Crashing through magic ruins for a death-defying jump that was just right, Crystal and her rescue team are about to embark on an epic quest to find a top secret magical...*thing*...and end this wicked winter. Stay tuned and stay toasty!"

Faybelle, watching the MirrorCast, had a sudden inspiration. "Whatever they are after sounds pretty important. I bet it would be worth a lot to the right fairies."

Meanwhile, Daring the Beast was trying to get in touch with Apple. He was throwing ice cubes at her dorm-room window. But when Apple opened the window, he accidentally bonked her in the head with one of his ice cubes.

"Hey! Do you mind?" she yelled before noticing who was throwing the ice cubes. "Daring?"

He looked up at her. His big, black nose was wet. His white fur was dingy. He'd never looked so sad. "I need a friend."

Daring climbed up to Apple's balcony, to Apple's surprise.

"Thanks, Apple," he said softly. "I know I must be hard to look at in this furry condition."

"No, I'm sorry," Apple said. "For what I said in the hall. I didn't mean to hurt your feelings."

Daring rubbed his face with his paw. "I'm sure this is just a temporary thing. I'll be gorgeous again."

Apple smiled sadly at him. "Or maybe our story is not what you thought it was. When I was in enchanted sleep, it didn't wake me. There was no magic."

"I can do better!" Daring promised. "Can I get a re-do?" He puckered up his polar-bear lips.

"You think if I let you kiss me again, you'll be my prince? I'm not even in peril right now."

"But I am!" blurted out Daring. "If we're meant to be together, maybe your kiss can save *me*."

Apple petted him softly. "It's worth a try."

She closed her eyes and waited. Daring the Beast slobbered her cheek like an overeager puppy. Nothing happened. Poor Daring.

Crystal, Ashlynn, Briar, and Blondie went up to Rosabella's

room to ask her about the Spring Rose and found her sitting with Daring the Beast. He was crying.

"The kiss was that bad?" Rosabella asked Daring.

"I'm a beast! My life is over!" he wailed.

Amazed, Crystal and her friends stared at him.

"What the hex?" exclaimed Ashlynn.

"What? You've never seen a cursed guy before?" Daring sobbed.

"It's Daring, you guys," explained Rosabella.

"That's new news." Blondie was delighted.

"Well, curses have been going around lately," realized Crystal.

The girls explained their quest for the four roses to Rosabella, and that they thought the Spring Rose would be at her castle.

"So, Rosabella," Briar asked, "are your folks okay with uninvited house guests?"

"Sure!" answered Rosabella. "That's pretty much how they met. I'd love to show you my home. Especially if a rose from there can cure curses. There's a huge rose garden. In fact, I know exactly where to start." She looked up at Daring. "Hey, why don't you come with us?"

He grinned. "You had me at *cures curses*!" His whiskers twitched happily.

"Just make yourself useful and don't be a royal pain," Rosabella said playfully.

He nodded—and his whiskers twitched happily again.

Rosabella blushed. But she had no idea why.

CHAPTER 20

Dashing Through the Snow

The girls were in front of the school, getting ready to leave on their quest. Their bags were packed and loaded onto Daring the Beast's back.

"I hate making myself useful," he complained.

From behind some snow sculptures, Faybelle was watching the preparations. She made a quick call to the Fairy Mob. "Okay, mob fairies, I have a proposal," she said in a hushed voice. "If I can get you something *hextremely* valuable, will you let me out of my debt?"

"I dunno. Whatcha got?" asked the head mobster.

"We don't really negotia-menate," added his buddy.

"How about a magic cure to the most ancient evil curse ever after?" Faybelle told them.

"We're listening," said the mobster. "You have three days. Or we double your duty."

The phone went dead.

Faybelle laughed ruefully. "No pressure." She ran over to the girls. She tossed her backpack to Daring. "Wait up, girls. I'm in!"

Briar was not surprised. "Faybelle has a thing about inviting herself," she whispered to Crystal. "Kind of part of our Sleeping Beauty story."

"Oh, come on," Faybelle said, laughing. "With Farrah taking a break, this crew needs a fairy. Don't you want to travel in style?"

With a wave of her hand, Faybelle created a lush sleigh for them to ride in.

"Not bad!"

"That's more like it!"

Faybelle smiled. "Hey, wait a spell. You wouldn't survive a day in this blizzard wearing those rags. How about something warmer?" She conjured beautiful, cozy new outfits for all the girls.

"It just needs one last thing," said Crystal. "You never can get enough sparkle!"

The girls climbed into the sleigh. *Uh-oh*, Daring realized. He was going to be pulling it! "When I called *the front*, this isn't what I had in mind!"

He started trudging up the icy road. Pulling the sleigh wasn't as hard as he thought, and soon he was galloping through the snow. The girls squealed behind him. They were off!

Jackie Frost and Northwind watched them leave.

"Crystal is trying to fix things herself," grumbled Jackie.

"But, Jackie, Crystal never does things for herself. That's why she has us servants."

"Had," Jackie corrected Northwind. "Our days of serving are done. But to make sure it stays that way, it looks like we're gonna have to close the book on Crystal's story ourselves. You're not getting cold feet, are you?"

Northwind laughed. "Kind of. Let's switch to claws!"

Jackie rolled her eyes. "Fine. Now, let's stop this rescue mission in its tracks!"

At that, Jackie and Northwind turned themselves into snowy owls and galloped after the sleigh.

CHAPTER 21

Spring into Spring

In the distance the girls could see the glimmering glory of Beauty and the Beast's castle. Rosabella had been telling them all about how beautiful the rose garden was in bloom. But when the sleigh came close to the grounds, the friends were horrified to see that the garden was completely dead, covered in a fine layer of newly fallen snow. The curse had reached even here.

Thorn-covered vines twisted over the crumbling walls. "You should see it in bloom," said Rosabella sadly.

"What if the Rose of Spring is dead?" Crystal said, worried.

Rosabella led them to a planter at the center of the garden. "It's not dead. It can't be," she said. "This is the most special rose here. The rose my father, the Beast, gave my mother the day she transformed him back into a prince. This was the rose I was named after."

"Spring's Rose stands out, all alone," Crystal said, remembering the words on the scroll.

But the rose was bare and thorny. It didn't even have any leaves on it, much less a blossom.

"It's not in season," said Briar.

Rosabella sighed. "So we have to wait until spring?"

"But spring isn't coming," Daring exclaimed. "We're *doomed*!"

The green eyes of two snowy owls peeked through a tangle of branches. Jackie and Northwind were watching everything.

Only Faybelle wasn't worried. "Step aside, Daring. Don't get your fur in a knot. I can help. Farrah Goodfairy isn't the only one who can make some major fairy magic!"

She hovered off the ground and began waving her arms like a cheerleader. "Two, four, six, eight. Roses, bloom, we cannot wait. Winter, spring, summer, fall. Bloom till we can't count them all!"

A delicate fragrance wafted through the air. Buds appeared. They began to unfurl and blossom. The whole garden filled with vibrant colors. Yellow roses. Pink roses. Purple roses. Faybelle floated even higher in the air, focusing on the special planter at the center. Rosabella and Daring stared transfixed as the rose began to bloom. It was bigger and more beautiful than any other in the garden. As the rose opened, red and radiant, the snow around them began to melt.

"Booyah!" shouted Faybelle gleefully. "And that's how fairy magic is done, people!"

Everyone applauded.

"Way to flip the script!"

"You did it!"

"Fairy nice work!"

"That's the Rose of Spring!"

"I'm impressed!"

Faybelle blushed; she was actually a little embarrassed by all the positive attention. After all, she did plan on betraying them. Even now her phone was buzzing. A quick glance showed the Fairy Mob on the line—but Faybelle declined the call with a quick press of her finger.

Far away on his balcony, the Snow King saw a tiny spot of color sprout in the distance. "What's this?" he wondered. "Who dares stain my perfectly blank landscape with that hideous color? I need a closer look!"

He turned his scepter into a telescope and gazed through it. Imagine the Snow King's surprise when he saw his daughter, Crystal, laughing with her friends in a springtime garden full of roses. He adjusted the telescope and focused on the central red rose, the biggest blossom of all.

"Just as I suspected. My daughter continues to defy me. But not for long!" The Snow King laughed wickedly.

One of the last frost elves in the palace cowered behind

him. But the elf already knew he was doomed. He held out his arms, prepared. With an angry zap, the Snow King turned him into, yes, another penguin.

No one was safe anymore from the Snow King's curses. The deep chill was freezing all the land.

CHAPTER 22

Winter Break

The girls and Daring the Beast gazed at the remarkable rose. Rosabella reached out and gently took it in her hands. "The Rose of Spring," she whispered. "I will guard it with my life."

"One down, three to go," said Crystal. "Thanks for your help, Rosabella."

Blondie was consulting her MirrorPhone, studying the photos of the scroll she'd taken. "According to the scroll of *Deep Magic*, the Summer Rose is at Cinderella's castle."

"Yay!" squealed Ashlynn, overjoyed to be home. "My place! You guys will love it."

"What are we waiting for? Let's get this snow on the road," Crystal exclaimed. But just as she was about to hop back on the sleigh, she noticed that her shoe-laces were untied. "Um, can someone help me lace up my boots?"

Her friends exchanged looks of confusion. Did she not know how to tie her laces?

Ashlynn was the first to find her voice. "Let me show you how to do it," she volunteered. "It's really easy. First, you grab both laces."

"Then grab the left over the right," explained Briar.

Crystal carefully followed their directions, surprised at how easy it was to tie her laces.

The evil-eyed snowy owl spying on the girls in the garden growled. "How adorable. Little Goody Two-skates trying to save her parents. Well, whatever she's up to, it won't work."

Jackie and Northwind crouched behind a bush as the sleigh whizzed past them.

Daring the Beast was grumbling. "My destiny turns out to be a lowly sled dog. *Ugh!*"

The clouds broke for a moment, and Crystal saw how low the sun was in the sky. Her curfew was approaching. She was supposed to be home soon. *But my dad is a danger to us all,* she thought. *I can't go back without a cure.*

When the sleigh had passed, Jackie and Northwind emerged, transformed back into elves. Jackie was curious about what the Snow King was up to. She pulled a snow globe out of her pocket and shook it. It pulsed and emitted a high-pitched buzzing.

At his castle, the Snow King was trying to dig out his sleigh from the snow. None of the servants could help him. They'd all been turned into penguins and seals, and they flapped their flippers behind him uselessly.

"Lazy servants," muttered the king. He was about to zap them all again when the snow globe on the top of his scepter began to pulse with light. It was ringing.

The penguins and the seals breathed a sigh of relief. They didn't know what might be worse than this—but they had a feeling the Snow King could make their lives even more miserable.

The Snow King answered his snow globe. "Well, well, Jackie Frost and Northwind! Where are you two? This isn't winter break!" The Snow King's eyes were flashing, and his face was red; he was even angrier than usual. "My daughter, Crystal, is out past curfew!"

Jackie covered her snow globe with her hand so the Snow King couldn't hear her. "We should probably go there and defeat him now," she whispered to Northwind.

"Maybe we should destroy him later. He's super busy."

Jackie nodded. "Yeah," she agreed. "Let him tire himself out. Then we take him down."

Jackie took her hand away from the snow globe and addressed the king. "Don't worry about Crystal, sire. We'll track down your daughter for you."

"Finally, some servitude!" shouted the Snow King into

the snow globe. "You find Crystal and tell her she hasn't just lost her right to the winter throne—she's *grounded*!"

Jackie Frost waited for the snow globe to click off. She cackled with glee. "Let's close the book on whatever Crystal is up to, then take care of the big guy. And then we rule!"

CHAPTER 23

Polar Paths

The blizzard was blinding. All anyone could see in any direction was a sea of swirling white. Daring trudged through deeper and deeper snow. The sleigh was barely moving. They were lost.

"Where are we, Crystal?" asked Ashlynn, trying to hide her panic.

"Not sure." Crystal sighed. "My MirrorPhone has no bars. We're out of range."

Daring the Beast's nose twitched. He sniffed the air. He sneezed. "I can't even smell which way to go. My nose is full of icicles!"

Briar shivered. "The only thing worse than being lost in the woods is being lost in the woods in the freezing cold."

Blondie looked at Crystal. "What do we do?"

"I don't know," Crystal admitted. "I've never made decisions before; they were always made for me."

Two winged shadows passed over the sleigh, but in their distress the girls barely noticed. Jackie and Northwind were disguised as snowy owls. They perched in a high tree and morphed back into elves. They sat like frosty gargoyles on a branch.

"Two paths to Cinderella's castle," noted Jackie, peering across the landscape. "One easy. One hard. And we're going to help them get there."

Northwind was confused. "Wait! I though we wanted to stop them."

Jackie laughed. "Duh! Watch and learn, snow bro. Crystal trusts us, so it's easy to trick her into telling us her plans. Then...*bam!* No more Crystal. Haha!"

Northwind shrugged. This didn't make much sense to him, but he was happy to change into an owl again with his sister. They flew together through the snow-covered trees and landed at a fork in the path. They changed back into cold, helpless elves.

"Rescue us!" Jackie cried as the sleigh approached.

"Help!" called Northwind, imitating his sister.

Crystal gasped, recognizing the elves. "I know them! That's Jackie Frost and Northwind. They work for my father."

Jackie ran over to the sleigh. "We were trying to escape the terrible anger of the Snow King," she cried to Crystal.

"You poor things!" Crystal's heart went out to them. "He's cursed, you know; it's not his fault!"

Crystal Winter lives happily ever after
in the Ice Palace with her parents,
the Snow King and Queen,
until Jackie Frost unleashes her
Kindness Blindness curse!

Crystal surprises her friends Briar Beauty and Ashlynn Ella at Ever After High and transforms the school into a spelltacular winter wonderland!

The cursed Snow King arrives at
Ever After High to find Crystal. When
Daring Charming refuses to help him,
the king turns Daring into an ice beast!

Jackie causes an avalanche to freeze the team in their tracks, but Crystal won't let anything get in their way!

Rosabella teaches Daring about caring for others.
Meanwhile, Faybelle schemes with the
Fairy Mobsters to avoid detention....

Crystal and her friends solve fairy tricky riddles to find the four enchanted roses at different fairytale castles.

Crystal wakes everyone up from the sleeping spell. They need to stop Jackie before she gets her hands on the Snow King's staff!

Crystal unites the four roses and breaks
the curse. The Epic Winter is over and
all of Ever After spellebrates!

"Oh, we totally know!" Northwind grinned. Jackie clapped her hand over his mouth.

"We were trying to seek refuge at Cinderella's castle," lied Jackie.

"Fableous!" said Crystal. "That's where we're going! The trouble is, we're a bit lost…"

"Whaddya know! I know the way!" Jackie smiled sweetly. "In fact, I know a shortcut."

As the elves hopped onto the back of the sleigh, Jackie leaned close to her brother. "This daddy's girl and her friends will never get their hands on the rest of this so-called curse cure. They're about to reach a dead end!" In a much louder voice, Jackie spoke to Crystal. "Turn right here!"

Daring the Beast veered toward a path that led up into the mountains. Snowy rock faces bounded the path on either side like bookends. Jagged peaks rose above them. The path looked more and more dangerous as they continued along it.

"Cinderella's castle is just over this rise," Jackie said.

"Careful, Daring," warned Crystal. "Move slowly. By the look of these hills, this is avalanche country."

"What?" Blondie asked in a booming voice. "Is that dangerous?"

"Shhh!" whispered Crystal. "Keep as quiet as you can. Loud noise can trigger an avalanche."

The girls looked nervously at the cliffs above them. Snow seemed to shift, and a fine white dust wafted through the air.

77

Jackie's eyes gleamed triumphantly. "That's right, Princess, it's a trap! You'll never see the Winter Palace again!"

"Jackie! Northwind!" Crystal didn't understand what she was hearing. "Why?"

Jackie laughed maniacally. "You're even easier to fool than your dad!"

"Surprise!" announced Northwind. "We put the curse on him!"

"Plot twist!" Faybelle hadn't expected this turn of events.

Crystal was indignant. "Traitors! You won't succeed. I'll stop you."

"Little Miss Can't-Even-Lace-Her-Own-Skates?" taunted Jackie. "You're clueless without your servants to do things for you. We won't serve anybody anymore! We're going to rule winter, and there's nothing you can do to stop us!"

Jackie opened her mouth and began to roar. She and Northwind were turning into polar bears! Their loud growls echoed back and forth. Avalanche!

Huge rolling waves of snow were crashing down the cliffs toward the sleigh. The girls were frozen in fear.

"Daring! Get us out of here!" begged Crystal.

Jackie and Northwind high-fived each other with their polar-bear paws. Success! They transformed into owls and flew high up into the sky.

Daring was galloping as fast as he could, but the wall of snow was gaining on them. The avalanche rumbled closer and closer. Jackie, peering down from the sky, watched the sleigh disappear into an ocean of whiteness. They were gone.

"Looks like Crystal's story is at *The End*," hooted Jackie. "C'mon. Let's get rid of the king of winter and finish this snow job!"

Jackie and Northwind swooped happily through the clouds. Their evil plan was working!

CHAPTER 24

Into Thin Air

A still sea of snow stretched between the peaks. All was eerily quiet—until Crystal's head popped up. One by one, the girls dug themselves out.

"Is everyone okay?" Crystal said, gasping. She checked to make sure they were all accounted for.

"Yes, I think so," Briar spluttered.

"Now I know how a Popsicle feels!" admitted Daring.

"There's snow in my underpants," complained Faybelle.

They had all survived—but the path to Cinderella's castle was blocked by snow.

"What do we do?" Ashlynn wondered aloud. "Going all the way around will take days."

"Days we don't have," said Briar.

Crystal was thinking out loud. "Jackie and Northwind

are headed to defeat my father and take over the Winter Palace. My family needs me now. We must push through."

"But how?" asked Blondie.

The sleigh was jammed into the top of a fifty-foot wall of snow. But Crystal was determined. "I am the princess of winter. I will not let a little wall of snow stop me."

"Um, excuse me," Daring the Beast interrupted. "But that's a super-*gigantic* wall of snow."

"Even if we make it over, and even if we get the roses we need from Cinderella's and Sleeping Beauty's castles, we still don't know where the final Rose of Winter is." Briar felt defeated.

"The world of Ever After is counting on us," Crystal reminded her. "This cannot be the end of the story. Did Jack give up when the Great Beanstalk was too tall? Did Rapunzel's prince look for a princess with shorter hair to climb? *No!*"

Still, the others looked stricken. Frustrated, Crystal looked down at her boots—the laces untied yet again. She took a big breath, tied them tight, and turned to her friends. They needed a pep talk. "We can do this! But only together. First, we gotta get our sleigh back."

Without turning around to see if the others were following, Crystal dug her hands into the ice wall. She was going to climb up it—without a harness.

"Is she really trying to climb that all by herself?" Daring chuckled.

"It's called *thinking of others*," Rosabella said pointedly. "She's worried about her family—about all of Ever After."

Rosabella looked up at her friend. "Hang on, Crystal. I'm with you!"

Crystal was digging her heels into the slick snow. She clutched jagged pieces of ice and hauled herself ever upward.

Blondie took out her MirrorPhone. She had to report on this story! "Crystal Winter, leading by example!"

Crystal glanced down and gave everyone a thumbs-up. She could do this. *Oops!* Her foot slipped, and she tumbled all the way back down the wall.

"Well, that's not going to work," mumbled Daring.

But Crystal had an even better idea. She'd noticed the giant icicles hanging from a jutting cliff above them. She pulled out her sparklizer from her backpack. First, she broke off the biggest icicle she could find. The other girls followed her lead and grabbed icicles of their own. Then Crystal shot an icicle at the wall of snow—it stuck, creating a step! She shot another icicle higher up. They could make an icicle ladder to the top! It was like a super-slippery climbing wall.

Daring went first. If it would hold his ice beast weight, it would hold them all. One after another, they clambered to the top—and to the sleigh.

The sky had cleared, and they could see in all directions. The view was exhilarating. Cinderella's castle sparkled in the valley just below them.

"It worked!"

"Oh, Crystal, I knew you could do it!"

"I'll give you points for that."

Crystal was pleased—and proud. She had solved the

problem all on her own. Still, it was no time to spellebrate. "We have to hurry and stop Jackie and Northwind," she reminded everyone.

Briar gulped. "But how do we get down?"

"*Ooh, ooh, ooh!* I know!" Daring raised his paw. "This is the fun part."

Daring picked up the reins of the sleigh. But he wasn't going to pull—he got on board, and everyone climbed in behind him. All they had to do was tip their weight forward just a little bit—and they were off! It was the sled ride of all sled rides!

They careened faster and faster and faster down the steep slope right toward the castle. Everyone was screaming! This was a blast! This was better than a roller coaster.

At the last minute, Daring reached out his paw and dragged it along the ground, until the sleigh skidded to a stop right at the castle entrance.

"*Owie!*" he moaned. He'd gotten a splinter in his paw.

"We made it!" Blondie sighed, relieved.

Briar looked at the steep stairs in front of them. "My poor feet cannot take another climb right now."

Ashlynn grinned and pressed a button on the side of the castle. It wasn't a staircase after all; it was an escalator. "My mom never wanted to lose a shoe on the run again," she explained to her friends.

As they floated up the moving stairs, the girls were awed at the beauty of the palace.

"Fableous," whispered Crystal.

Daring, however, was poking at his paw. He couldn't get the thorn loose—and it hurt. He tried not to whimper, but Rosabella noticed he was in pain.

"You hurt your paw," she said. "Let me see."

"No!" Daring pulled it away. "You can't touch it."

"Oh, don't be a big cub," Rosabella scolded him. "We'll find some bandages and fix you up, good as new."

CHAPTER 25

A Hint of Summer

Ashlynn led her friends through the grand entry of her home. Hallways led off in every direction. But much of the beauty of the palace was hidden beneath a thick layer of frost and ice and snow. Snowdrifts hugged the walls. Frost gleamed on the windows. The air was icy cold.

Everyone seemed to be gone. Cinderella and her subjects must have fled as the wicked winter settled in.

"We must find the Rose of Summer," said Crystal. "Ashlynn, does your mother have a place she keeps precious things?"

"Of course," answered Ashlynn assuredly. "She keeps the glass slipper in her bedroom shoe closet. We should check there first."

Rosabella told everyone to go on without her. She was

looking for a first aid kit. "Daring, come with me," she said as she headed down a hall that seemed to lead to the kitchen. "Let's get that splinter out of your paw."

In the kitchen, everything was made of glass. There were glass tables, glass chairs, gleaming glass countertops, and glassware. Rosabella threw open cupboard doors until she found what she was looking for. "Aha! A fairy first aid kit. *Heals like magic*," she read.

Daring winced as Rosabella poked his sore spot with tweezers. "*Ow! Ow!* Be careful, Rosabella!"

"Don't be a scaredy-beast," she told him.

"*Ow! Ow!* Just do it! *Oooh!*"

She was holding his paws in her hands. Their eyes met—and it was suddenly awkward. The thorn was out. His paw didn't hurt anymore.

"Oh…um…thanks," Daring stammered uncomfortably. "I don't know why you're so good to me. I mean, I'm not handsome anymore."

Rosabella looked into his eyes. "Daring, don't you know my legacy story? I see past what someone looks like on the outside. It doesn't matter if you're a handsome prince or a beast. It's what's inside that counts."

Daring breathed a sigh of relief. "I like your story."

Rosabella blushed, but she didn't look away. She was still holding his paw in her hand.

Up in Cinderella's magnificent bedroom, Ashlynn led the girls into her mother's enormous walk-in closet just for shoes. There were shelves from ceiling to floor, lined with hundreds of pairs of high heels, flip-flops, slip-ons, boots, and party shoes of all kinds. The girls were amazed.

"Welcome to Cinderella's shoe closet!" Ashlynn laughed. She gestured to a small vault at the back. "This is where my mom keeps her most valuable possessions. Only, it's locked."

Blondie examined the vault. "Locked, huh? I got skills!"

In a matter of moments Blondie had the vault open—but there was nothing inside except for the famous glass slipper.

"No Summer Rose," noted Blondie sadly.

"Is there a garden in the castle, perhaps?" Briar suggested.

Ashlynn shook her head. "No."

Faybelle's MirrorPhone rang. "This is not a good time," she hissed. It was the mob fairies.

"Your time is running out, toots," a gruff voice said.

Faybelle raised her voice to try and cover for the call. "I am interested in changing my service. Unlimited hext messaging, you say?" Faybelle excused herself and stepped into the hallway.

The phone call gave Ashlynn an idea. "I'll call Farrah Goodfairy. She knows our story as well as anyone. Maybe she'll know where the rose is."

Farrah was delighted to hear from the girls. "How's the

quest for a cure going?" she asked. She was in the Castleteria with Madeline and Apple.

"Fairy badly," Ashlynn admitted. "The Summer Rose is not in the slipper safe!"

"Hmmmm," mused Farrah. "It may be glamourized to look like something else."

"Then it could be anywhere!" Crystal cried. "And look like anything!"

Out in the hallway, Faybelle was listening to the mobsters' threats on her MirrorPhone. "You owe us for cleaning up your mess at Ever After. Now, you got an easy choice. Deliver the curse-curing goods you promised—and they better be good goods—or two hundred years of service."

"I'm working on it," Faybelle whispered sharply. "I can't steal what they haven't found yet."

While she was on her phone, Faybelle wandered down the hall. Without realizing it, she burst into the kitchen—where Daring the Beast and Rosabella were still holding hands...and paws.

"What's up?" Rosabella asked, breaking the romantic moment.

"Nothing," Faybelle lied. Her eyes narrowed as she took in the private scene. "What's up with you?"

"Nothing!" exclaimed Daring the Beast and Rosabella together.

Blondie poked her head in. "Breaking news, guys," she said. "The Summer Rose may be fairy glamourized. See anything weird or unusual in here?"

"Nope!" they all said together.

"Well, keep looking," Blondie ordered. Her reporter's instincts told her that *something* was up, however. All three of them were acting very suspicious.

But no one could find anything that might be the glamoured rose. They met up in the main hall a little while later. They were discouraged.

Ashlynn sighed. "We've looked everywhere!"

"*Hmmm*, what's that?" asked Blondie, pointing at a giant, round, orange object.

"It's the enchanted pumpkin from my story," explained Ashlynn, "the one that turned into a coach. But what's it doing here?"

Crystal's face lit up! "Maybe the pumpkin is the disguise in the riddle!"

Faybelle began doing jumping jacks and cheers. She was using her magic on the pumpkin. "One, two, three, four— fairy glamour hide no more!"

The pumpkin transformed—into a greenhouse!

"Yes!" Crystal pumped her fist in the air.

"Whoa!" exclaimed Ashlynn.

This was unexpected!

The greenhouse was lush with plants. There were beanstalks and all kinds of fairytale vegetables. Pumpkin vines crawled up the walls. In the very center of the greenhouse bloomed a single pink rose, grand and glorious.

Very carefully, Rosabella cut it from the stem and handed it to Ashlynn.

"I will keep the Summer Rose safe," Ashlynn promised solemnly.

Now they had two roses, but they still needed two more.

They all went back to the sleigh. It was time to head to Briar's family castle—the home of Sleeping Beauty.

CHAPTER 26

Hibernating!

Jackie and Northwind were tired. Flying was hard work! "We've flown halfway across the fairytale world," complained Northwind. "I need to switch from wings to legs for a while."

They landed and changed back into elves. As they began trudging through the deep snow, Jackie glared at her brother. This was better? At least they could cover more ground when they were owls.

Northwind's snow globe lit up. A call!

It was the cursed Snow King. He was in the wildest rage yet. "My daughter is out past her curfew," he screamed at Northwind. "Yet I see her running from castle to castle with her little friends while you two flit around like a couple of winter pixies!"

The Snow King had been watching everything through his telescope. He slammed down the snow globe, and the line went dead.

"But this is impossible!" Jackie moaned. She thought they had stopped Crystal. "I've underestimated the princess for the last time. No more playing nice."

"You were playing nice?" Northwind was totally confused.

"She can't get another step closer to this so-called cure," Jackie ranted. "We have to beat her to Sleeping Beauty's castle. Then..."

"Then what?" Northwind chuckled. "We tuck her in for a nice, long nap?"

"Northwind, you idiot!" But Jackie paused. Maybe that wasn't such a stupid idea after all. "You're brilliant. Sleeping Beauty's spindle! Don't you know your fairytale history? I totally have a plan. Let's go!"

She turned back into an owl. With a tired sigh, Northwind joined her in the sky.

Daring the Beast was pulling the sleigh again. Bells jingled as they raced across the frozen landscape.

"I can't wait to see your castle, Briar," Crystal said to her friend. "I'm a big fan of your story."

"I dunno," Ashlynn admitted. "Enchanted sleep for one hundred years sounds exhausting!"

"Sleeping Beauty's story is about more than sleep," explained Briar. "There's magic and romance and—"

"And a wicked awesome villain, if I do say so myself," Faybelle butted in. Her mother was the Evil Fairy in that story. "Look! There's the castle! Let's get that rose!"

The sleigh glided up to the castle. It was completely covered in thousands of beautiful roses—and each and every rose was covered in ice.

"I guess the gardeners took off at the first frost." Briar gulped.

Crystal recited from memory the words on the scroll: *"The Rose of Fall hides in the crowd."*

Ashlynn voiced everyone's concern. "But which rose is the Fall Rose? There are a million flowers!"

Crystal was trying to put together the clues. There was some detail from the fairytale that would help them figure this out. "Every season's rose has been tied in some way to the origin story from that castle. In Sleeping Beauty's, maybe it's in your mom's bedroom, where she slept for a hundred years?"

"No!" said Faybelle. She knew the story better than anyone besides Briar. "There's another room far more important to our story. Isn't there, Briar?"

Briar looked frightened. "But it's forbidden. The magic spinning wheel is locked away in the tower." She pointed to the very highest turret of the castle.

"Sounds like that's where we'll find the rose," Crystal decided. "Let's go."

But they couldn't open the doors to the castle. Daring used all his brute strength, but they wouldn't budge.

"Uh, Daring," interrupted Briar, "I've got this." She lifted a garden pot and picked up a spare key.

"Oh, sorry!" Daring apologized. "My bad."

The doors swung open and they entered the main hall—a circular room with a staircase that wound round and round up to the turret. Briar Beauty was trembling.

"Briar, you don't have to come if you're too afraid," said Faybelle. But Briar was confident and she headed for the stairs.

Vines grew up the walls and the banisters. It was a jungle of twisting branches, tangled roots, and roses—roses everywhere. The staircase was blocked by dense overgrowth. Daring used his claws like a machete to slash an opening, but it was no use. The foliage was too thick.

"Holy roses!" Daring said. "Where's an enchanted Weedwacker when you need one?"

"We'll never get up to the tower through this!" cried Briar, looking at the prickly vines.

But Crystal was studying the vines. She thought there might be another way. "Maybe we don't have to get through. We can use these vines as a shortcut right to the top. Watch."

Crystal blasted the ice and snow off a central vine dangling high above them. Without the weight of the snow, the vine sprang up and down like a bungee cord. Crystal grinned.

"Whoa! Going up!" Ashlynn grabbed hold of a vine and whizzed to the top of the turret. It was like the scariest, most fun thrill ride at an amusement park.

"What a rush!" hollered Daring the Beast. "Everyone's got to try that!"

They all swung to the very tip-top of the turret. Her hands shaking with fear, Briar opened the door to the attic room. This is where her mother's great sleep had begun when she pricked her finger on the spinning wheel.

Snow covered the old, broken furniture, but there were no roses in this room. It was quiet, dead, and cold. A shaft of light from the window fell on the dreaded spinning wheel.

"Ah, porridge!" Blondie cursed. "This is the one place roses aren't."

Briar was mesmerized by a basket of golden, fluffy wool next to the spinning wheel. It was the most beautiful thing she had ever seen. As if in a trance, she approached the spindle.

"It's her fairytale," Faybelle explained. "Touch the spindle, go to sleep. She can't help herself."

Faybelle couldn't help herself, either. After all, this was her story, too. "Double-dare you to touch the spindle," she taunted Briar.

Slowly, Briar reached out her hand.

"Stop!" shouted Crystal as loudly as she could. She grabbed Briar's hand before it touched the deadly spindle.

Faybelle blushed and laughed. "I was only kidding," she said, pretending.

"Magic wool," noted Crystal, picking up a strand. "The rose at Cinderella's castle was protected by magic. Maybe the Rose of Fall is, too."

Crystal, who was in no danger of pricking her finger, sat down at the spinning wheel with the golden wool. She began turning the spindle. Round and round it went—but it wasn't spinning thread; it was creating a glowing yellow rose!

Blondie gasped. "News flash! This just in! We've found the Rose of Fall!"

Very carefully, Briar picked the rose from the spinning wheel. "The Rose of Fall is safe with me."

Now three of the girls had their magical roses.

"That was close, Briar," said Faybelle, trying to sound friendly. "If you had touched that spindle, it would have been a hundred-year snooze."

"Think again, Faybelle," announced a voice.

Two snowy owls were perched on the window ledge. The larger one, Jackie, flew over and settled on the spinning wheel. Northwind flapped his wings in the girls' faces. Then both birds transformed back into frost elves.

"I think it's time *all* you meddling fools took a long winter's nap!" Jackie threatened.

"Sweet dreams!" cackled Northwind.

Jackie and Northwind wrapped their scarves over their faces while Jackie reached out and broke the cursed spindle. She snapped it in half! An explosion of magic dust filled the room. The girls gasped and struggled to breathe. Jackie scooped a little of the magic spindle dust into an envelope and closed it.

The girls staggered wearily. They were just so tired. They were falling asleep on their feet. Daring the Beast was already starting to snore.

"I do believe I have the vapors," he muttered as he dozed off with the others.

"Princess," Jackie whispered to Crystal, "your little plan has backfired."

"You…are…wicked." Those were Crystal's last words before drifting into a deep slumber.

She and her friends were all sound asleep.

"But, Jackie, won't they freeze, sleeping in the snow?" worried Northwind.

"That's the best part!" Jackie giggled. "Come, Northwind—we have a king to crush."

But something didn't feel right to Northwind. Before turning back into an owl, he glanced one more time at the kids sleeping in the snow. But what could he do? This was part of the plan, wasn't it?

The two owls spread their wings. It was time to return to the Snow King.

CHAPTER 27

Sweet Dreams

All the servants and courtiers at the palace had been turned into arctic animals. Penguins huddled in frozen clusters as far away from the Snow King as they could get. The castle was very quiet. No one was laughing or talking. The seals were careful not to bark. There was no one for the king to talk to. There wasn't even anyone to get angry at anymore.

The Snow King turned to his frozen wife. "I don't know, my dear. I'm beginning to question if I've been seeing things clearly."

An owl hooted. "Hey, *Mister Cool*!"

The king whirled around, enraged at the insult. "*Mister?* It's *sire* or *Your Highness*," he bellowed.

But Jackie was ready. She morphed into her elf self, her

hand already on the pouch of sleeping crystals she'd collected from the broken spindle. She blew them through a straw—right at the king's face.

The Snow King staggered backward, swinging his scepter wildly. The penguins and the seals slid to safety across the ice-covered floor.

The Snow King teetered. He tottered. He yawned. He leaned against his scepter and fell asleep on his feet.

"Nighty-night, *Your Highness*," mocked Jackie triumphantly.

"How dare you..." the king muttered in his sleep.

"Northwind! Grab his staff!" Jackie ordered.

But Northwind could not pry the scepter clutched in the king's hands free. It was as if they were frozen together.

"It's always something" fretted Jackie. Without the scepter, she could not rule winter. She had to find some way to get it!

Crystal and all her friends were lost in a deep, enchanted slumber.

Snow fell on them and they didn't notice. Their lips turned blue, but they didn't feel it. Each of them was somewhere else, in their very own dreamland.

Briar dreamed that she was in the Spindle Room—only it was summer, and the air was warm. She was about to touch the spindle, but Faybelle stopped her and turned it into a butterfly that flew away.

Ashlynn dreamed she was at the top of the stairs at her

mother's castle. Ashlynn ran down the stairs and lost her slipper along the way—but she just floated down to Hunter Huntsman in a sparkling ball gown.

Blondie Lockes dreamed she was at the Three Bears' cottage deep in the woods. Momma Bear had cooked up a banquet of delicious desserts and invited Blondie to sit at the family table and taste each sugary sweet.

Rosabella dreamed that Daring was lost in the woods, surrounded by wolves. But she leaped into action. Rosabella understood the wolves weren't evil and calmed them. Daring was inspired by how selfless Rosabella was, and he turned into the handsome prince he once was—and they kissed.

Crystal dreamed she was home at the Winter Palace and her parents were themselves again. Her smiling mother and her happy father led her to the throne. The Snow Queen placed a crown on her head. The Snow King handed her the Winter Rose. She stared and stared at the rose. Something was the matter. What was it?

In her dream, Crystal remembered that the Snow King was being controlled by Jackie and Northwind. "Dad," she screamed.

"Crystal," shouted her father. "You have to wake up!"

In the Spindle Room, Crystal tossed and turned. She couldn't wake up. She was under a spell! But she had to. She willed herself to. Her eyes blinked open.

Daring the Beast was curled up asleep in a basket. All the other girls were lost in dreamland still. Struggling to keep her eyes open, Crystal crawled to the spindle. She took the broken pieces and bound them together with golden wool. The sleeping dust was no longer spilling into the room.

Crystal shouted, "Wake up, Briar! Faybelle! Blondie! Everyone!"

They yawned and stretched. They opened their eyes.

"I know where the Rose of Winter is!" Crystal announced when they were all awake.

But they had to act fast.

CHAPTER 28

Twister!

*E*ven in his slumber, the dreams of the Snow King were controlling the wicked winter weather. As the Snow King snored and grumbled, he clutched his magical staff protectively. Snow fell in the throne room—and in his bad dreams, blizzards whirled.

The wicked winter was becoming wilder and wilder.

Huge snowballs landed like bombs all around Sleeping Beauty's castle. The winds twisted into tornadoes. The sleigh was still parked at the entrance—but how would they get to it?

"We are doomed!" worried Ashlynn. "Is this *The End*?"

"This is *news*! My chance to be a real field reporter!" Blondie said, setting up for her MirrorCast. "Hello, Ever After!

This is Blondie Lockes, reporting live. You've probably noticed we are facing some fairy twisted weather."

"I have to get up to the top of the world fast," said Crystal. "I have an idea how, but you have to trust me. Everyone, get on the sleigh. Daring, we need a push."

The others were a little nervous, but they climbed aboard.

"Won't we get swept up by the tornados if we try sledding now?" Daring the Beast asked.

"I'm counting on it," explained Crystal. "Everybody, hang on. Now, Daring, now! Hang on, friends!"

Daring gathered his strength and pushed the sleigh into the whirling tornado. He leaped onto the back at the last minute. The sleigh was spinning up, up, up in the air!

"Whoooooooah!"

"Hang on tight!"

"This is not just right!"

"My hair!"

They rocketed skyward. Daring lost his grip and flew off, only his ankle attached to the sleigh by a loose rope. The girls hauled him back in.

"We haven't faced our biggest challenge yet," shouted Crystal into the wind. "It's time to storm the castle!"

The twister spun them round and round. They were headed to the top of the world!

CHAPTER 29

Back to the Winter Palace

The blizzard brought its frostbitten fury to the farthest reaches of the land of fairytales. Would the world be buried under snow forever?

At Ever After, shivering trolls huddled under bridges. The geese could no longer make their deliveries. Fairy folk sought out any warmth they could find—from the sputtering lights of candles to the tiny glows of lamps. Townspeople fled to the castle school seeking refuge. They huddled under blankets in the hallways. They were all freezing.

Baba Yaga brewed up mug after mug of hot cocoa, and Headmaster Grimm served them in the auditorium. The screen above the stage displayed Blondie's Mirror-Cast. Everyone was following the girls' quest for the curse cure. Their only hope for relief from the winter was the Snow Princess and her friends struggling to the top of the world.

The sleigh corkscrewed inside the snow twister—up, up, up, and round, round, round. The girls hung on for dear life.

"Not much longer!" gasped Crystal.

"Yeah, not much longer till I'm sick!" Faybelle moaned.

The sleigh shot out the top of the tornado above the storm clouds. The stars were shining. The sky was clear. The green and gold lights of the aurora borealis twinkled over the Snow King's castle. No longer held up by the wild winds, the sleigh careened through the air—and crash-landed in a snowbank.

"Don't worry! I'm fine," said Daring, staggering dizzily to his feet.

"The Winter Palace!" Crystal exclaimed. "I'm home again."

"Now all we have to do is get there," added Daring. The castle was still far away across a snow-white plain, and the sleigh was smashed to smithereens.

"And we have to stop Jackie Frost and her brother, Northwind." Rosabella shook the snow out of her hair.

"And find the Rose of Winter," Ashlynn reminded them.

Briar nodded. "And remove the curse from Crystal's parents."

"Then save the world of Ever After from eternal winter!" Crystal was not going to let herself feel defeated. "That's everything, right? So what are we waiting for?"

"How about a ride?" Faybelle suggested. She pointed out the broken sleigh.

But Crystal was examining the splintered wood. She had an idea! A powerful idea.

Northwind was still trying to figure out how to get the scepter out of the sleeping Snow King's clutches. He noticed Crystal and her friends approaching the Winter Palace through the king's sceptor.

"Uh, Jackie." Northwind coughed nervously, trying to get his sister's attention. "'Member how you said Crystal would sleep for a hundred years and we would never see her again?"

Jackie looked up, irritated. "Yes, Northwind." The tiny elf was lounging on the throne.

"Well," Northwind continued, "either you were wrong or a hundred years goes by really fast. She's here, at the top of the world."

Jackie leaped up and scurried out to the balcony to see for herself. "Huh! I didn't think she had it in her. She's still just an overprivileged princess. She can't actually *do* anything. You know why? Because we got the palace, and who has the power? We've got the power! We won! And if the pampered princess can actually make it to the palace, we'll deal with her then."

Northwind was still tugging at the scepter. At last, he asked his sister something that had been troubling him. "What exactly will we rule if the world gets destroyed by winter?"

Jackie glared at him, and he put the thought out of his mind. "You're so smart," he complimented her. "I guess you've got it all figured out."

But Crystal was the one who had a real plan. She had turned the remains of the sleigh into cross-country skis for all of them!

"A powerful plan, Princess!" Rosabella praised Crystal. "We'll fly across the snow!"

"Nice idea," said Faybelle with a flutter of her wings. "I'll just fly."

"Could someone help me with this knot?" Crystal asked, tying her bootlaces again. "I promise, I almost have it."

Ashlynn leaned in to lend a hand. As soon as she was done, they were off!

Back at the castle, Jackie had no time to lose. She had to get the Snow King's scepter!

"C'mon! Ugh!" She struggled, pulling at it.

Northwind added his hands to hers. They pushed, they shoved, they pulled—and finally they did it! With a crack, the staff skittered across the icy floor!

"Oh yeah!" shouted Jackie. "I am awesome!"

"Nothing can stop us now!" Northwind clapped his hands happily. He skidded across the ice toward the scepter—and bonked his head on a column.

No longer supported by his scepter, the king toppled over and landed at the feet of the frozen queen. He snored even louder. Jackie stuck the king's thumb in his mouth to silence him and then grabbed the scepter.

"At last!" she exclaimed. "The power of winter!"

Northwind rubbed the side of his aching head. "Well, you'd better use it quick to turn off the wicked weather down below. 'Cause if the world gets buried, who do we get to boss around?"

Jackie strode out to the balcony. She was just barely tall enough to see over the railing. She aimed the scepter at the giant blizzard's swirling clouds. "Begone!"

A huge blast shot out of the scepter—and boomeranged right back at her, knocking her off her feet. Something was wrong!

Northwind looked through the telescope. "Whoa! You just, like, doubled it! Snowflakes the size of houses! That was your plan, right? I'm confused."

"Yeah, of course I meant to do that," said Jackie sarcastically.

But Northwind didn't catch her tone. "You are so smart!"

he told his sister. "This plan is so tricky I can't even tell how it will work at all!"

Jackie studied the staff in her hands. It had powers she didn't understand. Would she be able to figure out how to control it before Crystal arrived at the Winter Palace? She'd better....

CHAPTER 30

The Blizzard of the Century

No one at Ever After High could believe it! The blizzard was worse! A single giant snowflake that looked like a circular saw sliced off the top of one of the towers. Kids were panicking. The castle was shaking.

Back at the Winter Palace, Jackie was fiddling with the scepter to see if she could figure out how to work it. "Let me adjust a few settings," she muttered to herself.

She clicked a button, and a blast of magic ice shot out of the top of the staff. Northwind ducked just in time. The column behind him was shattered.

"Just testing the range," said Jackie, trying to hide her worried expression. "By the time Crystal walks up to the gates, I'll be ready."

Faybelle was leading everyone, flying just ahead to scout out the path. Her phone began buzzing, and she rolled her eyes, furious. "Hello?" she answered, trying to come up with a quick cover. "People for the Ethical Treatment of Unicorns?" She turned to the skier behind her. "I've got to take this call."

Faybelle flew ahead and darted behind a snowbank for privacy.

"The Fairy Mobfather is thinking you are avoiding your commitment to two hundred years of hard labor," growled the mobster on the phone.

"No, no, no!" Faybelle protested. "I just need a bit more time. What I have to trade is *ancient magic!*"

"You have this wit you now?"

Faybelle cleared her throat. "Not exactly, but I will!"

"Yeah, you will," chuckled the mobster. "By five o'clock today, or else we double the years of service!"

The mob fairies hung up. Faybelle was outraged. "Double?" she fumed.

The others came around the corner. "Double, uh, my donation," she covered. "Nothing is too good for those sweet, lovely unicorns. Thanks! Bye!"

Ashlynn smiled at her. "I didn't know you liked unicorns so much."

"Oh, you know me!" Faybelle laughed lightly. "I am so full of surprises."

Rosabella stopped in her tracks. "You guys go ahead," she said. "My ski is falling apart."

"I could carry you," offered Daring the Beast. He held out a paw.

Rosabella couldn't believe it. "Are you finally thinking of something other than yourself?"

"Why, no!" Daring was confused. "I was thinking that you might enjoy hearing some stories of my greatest exploits..."

She sighed. "When will you ever change?" But she climbed onto his back and they loped off together.

Before long the group was at the gates to the Winter Palace.

Jackie was watching. "The princess returns. Well, we have a little welcome planned for her!"

She aimed the staff, but when she tried to fire it, it blasted her in the face with a snowball.

"Awesome!" Northwind complimented her. "Welcome her with a snowball!"

"No, Northwind!" shouted Jackie, irritated. "You are the welcoming committee. Go down to the main hall and stop them. I will be sitting on the throne. Someone has to."

"Cool! All part of the plan! Wait. How do I stop them?"

"You are a shapeshifter!" Jackie's face was red with fury. "Use your power!"

Northwind looked scared. "All by myself? I'm afraid. There's a lot of them, and they have a beast!"

Jackie looked at her staff. It was glowing. "And you have the power of *ice*!" She pointed the scepter at her brother. She blasted him with the staff.

"Awesome!" said Northwind, sounding relieved.

"Show our princess what epic power looks like!" said Jackie with a smile.

But while they were talking, Jackie and Northwind didn't see two winter pixies sneaking behind the thrones! Crystal's wand was glowing under her throne.

CHAPTER 31

Snowball Fight

Daring the Beast opened the palace doors. He and the girls entered cautiously.

"Great work, Daring," said Crystal courageously. "Now let's get to the throne room and find that Rose of Winter. But watch out for—"

"For me!" Northwind leaped in front of Daring the Beast. "That's right. Turn back, by order of the new queen of winter, my sister, Jackie."

Daring the Beast chuckled. "Okay. I got this."

He roared as loudly as he could. He looked over his shoulder to grin at the girls—and didn't see what happened next. Northwind transformed himself into a fifty-foot-tall ice giant!

"Run!" screamed Crystal.

The girls raced for cover behind huge pillars of ice. The ice giant grabbed Daring and lifted him up in the air.

"Not the face! Not the face!" cried Daring, covering his head with his paws.

"Ho! Ho! Ho!" Northwind laughed, delighted. "Behold the power of winter!"

Crystal stepped forward. "Northwind! Nobody should get hurt for my sake! We're only here to save my parents! Please! Put him down!"

"My sister says you just give orders!" Northwind mocked her. "Pampered princess."

A snowball flew through the air—and hit Northwind on the nose!

"The princess said put him down!" It was Rosabella. "That wasn't an order! But call it a strong suggestion!"

She flung another snowball at Northwind, and he batted at her. Daring struggled free until only his tail was in Northwind's fist. He wriggled until he dropped to ground—and raced over to Rosabella.

"Hey, Northwind," shouted Crystal. "You like frozen fireworks?" She told the girls to split up so he couldn't go after them all at once.

"Fee, fie, fo, fum!" Northwind bellowed, trying to sound like a real giant. "Always wanted to say that! I'm gonna getcha!"

From behind a pillar, Blondie pulled out her MirrorPad and began broadcasting an update. "Will Crystal Winter be able to get to the throne room to find the final rose? Will she get her destiny back from the villainous Jackie Frost? Will—" In midsentence she suddenly screamed!

Back at Ever After High, everyone was watching the MirrorCast on the big screen in the auditorium. What was happening?

Northwind was stomping toward Ashlynn and Briar.

"Over here!" called Crystal, trying to distract him. "I'm the one you want."

Northwind spun around. He charged toward Crystal, who started to run—but tripped over her untied laces!

"Daring, we have to do something!" said Rosabella. "Let's go!"

Together, Daring and Rosabella raced in front of Northwind to block his path.

"That's far enough!" announced Rosabella bravely.

"Whoa!" gasped Daring the Beast, staring at Northwind's ice giant feet. "Those just might be the largest feet I have ever seen!"

Northwind looked down. "Cool, huh? Actually, it's my first time becoming an ice giant. Pretty awesome, if I do say so myself."

"You are gigantic!" Daring complimented him expertly.

"Crystal, run," whispered Rosabella. "Get up to the throne room. Daring and I have got this. I don't know how, but somehow we've got this!"

Crystal nodded gratefully. "Stay safe. Everyone else, come with me!"

"Very impressive, my man," continued Daring the Beast.

The girls began to sneak through the main hall with Crystal.

"But hardly the *most* impressive," Daring added.

Rosabella smiled at him. "Keep it up!" she told him.

"What?" He was confused.

"Distracting the giant!" replied Rosabella.

But the spell was broken. Northwind realized what had happened. "Hey! I'm not *that* dumb!" he said. But it was too late. The girls had already made it past him.

CHAPTER 32

Battle on Ice

ackie was still trying to figure out how to use the Snow King's magical scepter. She fired it at a pillar, missed, and tried again. This time she hit it. "Aim, ice," she told herself. "That's more like it. Jackie rules!"

Suddenly, there was a call on the globe atop the scepter. Jackie answered it. "Is it too much to ask if you have defeated the little princess and her pompous pack of minions?"

Northwind leaned into view. "Oh, we are totally winning," he told his sister confidently. "Except that Crystal and her friends got away and are heading toward you."

"AAAAGH!" Jackie screamed. "What part of that is *winning*? Okay, I'm doing this myself."

Jackie turned her attention to the Snow King and Snow Queen. She knew Crystal was after the last rose, the

Rose of Winter. Jackie plucked it from the queen's hand and froze it to her own collar. "She's going to have to get through me first," she cackled.

Crystal appeared a moment later, flanked by her friends. Jackie was on the throne. Blondie was filming the whole scene so that everyone at Ever After High could follow what was happening.

The first thing Crystal saw was her parents—asleep and frozen. "Mom! Dad!" she called. "Jackie Frost, you'd better not have hurt them!"

"They're fine," sneered Jackie. "And I'll do whatever I want. I'm the boss around here. Not you!"

"But this is not your palace! You stole it!" Crystal was outraged.

Jackie mocked her. "Boo-hoo-hoo!"

"The staff of winter!" Crystal realized Jackie was holding it. "It is too dangerous! The people and creatures of Ever After are being buried by this wicked winter! I know how to use the staff!"

While she was talking, the winter pixies crept out from under the throne, carrying Crystal's wand.

"You don't know anything," answered Jackie angrily. "You can't do anything. You don't deserve power. You just consider winter your playground. Fun, fun, fun. Some of us do *all* the work!"

"Winter should be fun," Crystal responded. "And yes, it is work to prepare a good winter. But we should be working together. All of us doing our best..."

Jackie didn't want to hear any more of this. She leaped up, brandishing the staff. The pixies startled and jumped back. "You? The next queen of winter? Ha!"

"Because I care!" Crystal stood up to Jackie. "I care about all the creatures of winter. Because I've struggled. Because I've climbed ice walls. I quested to find a cure for my parents. I crossed the world. I risked everything to get back what I had once upon a time. I understand what a great responsibility this is, and I am ready—not to rule, but to serve."

"You tell her!" cheered Blondie.

The students and teachers listening to this speech at Ever After High nodded in agreement. The penguins in the throne room cheered!

Jackie scoffed at Crystal's inspiring message. "You want to use the immense power of winter to help others? Girl, I always thought you were a bit weird."

"Jackie, please, give me the staff." Crystal extended her hand. "Let me heal winter, for everyone."

Crystal was approaching Jackie, one slow step at a time. Jackie's eyes were narrowed, glaring at the princess. Ashlynn and Briar hugged each other. Faybelle was shocked. Blondie was filming everything.

"Jackie's going to blast-freeze Crystal," worried Faybelle. She was right.

CHAPTER 33

The Big Chill

Northwind wasn't used to his new size. He staggered after Rosabella and Daring, waving his enormous hands at them—and missing every time.

"Gotcha! Er, no, I don't."

"How much longer do we have to play this game of cat and mouse?" Daring panted, out of breath.

Rosabella's eyes widened. That was it! "Daring, you're brilliant!"

He grinned. "Yes, well, thank you . . . How?"

Rosabella was thinking fast. "Northwind is a shapeshifter, right? All we have to do is get him into a different shape."

Far above them, Northwind couldn't hear what they were whispering. Daring stepped out from behind a pillar. "Say, Northwind, old chap, Rosabella and I were just wondering…well, this is awkward…but I say that you can choose any winter creature to shape-shift into."

"That's right, I can!" bragged Northwind.

Daring cleared his throat, stalling for time. "But, well, um, Rosabella here…"

"I say that Daring is wrong! You can't," Rosabella teased Northwind. Daring stepped in front of her protectively.

Northwind was offended. He puffed out his chest. He roared!

"But I'm on your side, old boy!" said Daring hastily. "Let me see, you were a polar bear, and, um, an owl…"

Northwind transformed in an instant to a snowy owl! "I do that one good! See?"

"Yeah!" Daring complimented him. "And a snow mouse!"

Rosabella shook her head. "He was never a mouse," she insisted.

"Yes, I was!" protested Northwind. "Wasn't I?"

Daring sighed. "That's the problem. I say yes, and she says no."

"Northwind can turn into whatever Northwind wants to!" the snowy owl announced. An instant later, he squeaked. He was a tiny, tiny mouse.

"Now, Daring!" shouted Rosabella.

Daring leaped, catlike, onto the mouse and pinned him with his giant paws. The game was over.

Rosabella clapped her hands. "Gotcha!"

Northwind was strangely unworried. "I'm guessing that

this is all part of Jackie's plan," he said mysteriously, his mouse whiskers twitching.

Needless to say, it wasn't. Jackie was facing off with Crystal in the throne room.

"Jackie, do the right thing," Crystal urged her. "Give me the staff. Give me the Rose of Winter. You do not have the power to control it. You will only get hurt!"

"Pretty words from a pretty useless princess," Jackie taunted her. She spun the staff in her hands, and it began to glow.

Crystal shook her head, concerned. "A stolen destiny will never give you a Happily Ever After. Join me!"

"What if I do?" asked Jackie. "Why should I?"

"You know I have no powers," Crystal told her. "My dad took them away. I stand before you humbly to ask you to turn back. Join me! Heal the world!"

No one dared to move. The kids in the auditorium at Ever After High all held their breaths. Would Jackie take Crystal's offer?

But Faybelle wasn't going to wait to find out! Quick as a flash, she flew toward Jackie—and snatched the Rose of Winter from her jacket. Jackie spun around. She shot a beam of slush toward Faybelle and froze her in midair! Faybelle, holding the Rose of Winter, was a solid block of ice. She clunked to the floor.

"I knew it was a trick!" screeched Jackie.

"No, Jackie!" Crystal wailed.

"You think you are a big deal," sneered Jackie. "Well, I

can be a big deal, too." She began to entice the magic energy out of the staff. Purple and pink lights flickered around her. She grew taller and taller and taller until she was as tall as the ceiling. She was an ice giant! "Now it's time to end this story, starting with your parents."

Jackie aimed the magic staff at the king and queen, but Crystal dived in front of them. "No!" She tripped. Her laces were untied again.

The winter pixies raced to protect her.

Jackie laughed. "You want to join her? Then you share her fate."

But she didn't know that one of the pixies had slipped Crystal her wand!

"My wand of winter!" Crystal whispered.

Just as Jackie went to blast her, Crystal created a shield around her parents, the pixies, and herself. Jackie couldn't even see them anymore! The jolt of frost she'd fired formed a circle of ice around the shield.

"What?" Jackie was baffled.

Behind the shield, Crystal used the wand to enchant a small pile of snow. The pixies pulled her parents to safety behind their thrones.

Crystal stepped out from behind the shield, wand raised. "You want to play? Let's play!"

What she'd forgotten to do was tie her laces. The strings straggled on either side of her shoes. What if she tripped again?

Ashlynn and Briar watched from afar, terrified.

Jackie cackled. "Play? Ha! Come back when you've learned to tie your own—"

But Crystal had already done it! She knew how! She'd tied her laces and her boots transformed into skates. "I've learned a whole lot on this adventure."

Crystal turned her wand into a hockey stick, just as she had long, long ago with her father. She conjured a hockey puck with a puff of frozen breath, just as her mother had done. Crystal hit it with her stick right at Jackie's feet. She zigged and zagged across the icy floor. The puck ricocheted—and walloped Jackie on the nose!

Jackie, unused to her giant size, lumbered across the room. But Crystal was too fast for her. Jackie swung the staff wildly, blasting here and there. Ice was spraying everywhere. Icebergs hardened in the room. Jackie had frozen her own feet to the floor! She bellowed and struggled, but she couldn't move.

Clutching each other, Ashlynn and Briar breathed a sigh of relief. Faybelle tried to cheer from inside her block of ice. The crowd at Ever After High went wild.

Crystal skated gracefully. She twirled in the air and landed cleanly on one foot, her other leg stretched behind her. Everyone applauded!

"Crystal Winter is on fire!" Blondie reported.

"Hey, Jackie!" Crystal called, and fired the hockey puck right at her. The princess skated full speed in Jackie's direction. She created an ice arch, just as she had done when she played with her father. It went right up the side of the frozen ice giant. Crystal whizzed up it and knocked the staff from Jackie's grip. Without the magic staff, Jackie shrank back to normal size. Crystal froze her hands with blocks of ice.

"Not fair!" Jackie whined.

With a gentle push, Crystal slid the frozen elf across the room—right into the hockey net.

"Goal!" shouted Blondie. "What an upset!"

"You get to stay there until you learn to chillax," Crystal told Jackie.

With Jackie's powers gone, Faybelle's ice cube began to melt, and soon she was free. Daring and Rosabella rushed into the room. Northwind, in Daring's paws, squeaked. Crystal bound him in ice as well and dropped him next to his sister.

He giggled. "Hi, Jackie. Is this part of the plan, too? You're so clever!"

His sister rolled her eyes. "Ugh!"

On orders from Crystal, a troop of penguins lifted the frozen elves and carried them out of the room. Enough. It was time to put them on ice and make sure they couldn't get into any more trouble!

CHAPTER 34

❧

The Greatest Magic of All

*C*rystal's quest was over at last. She and her friends had found all four magic roses. As they brought the roses together in the center of the room, the flowers began to glow. They floated out of the girls' hands, and their stems twisted together to form a bouquet.

"We can finally cure the Kindness Blindness." Ashlynn was relieved.

But Faybelle's fingers were still wrapped around the Rose of Winter.

"Faybelle?" Crystal questioned.

For a moment, guilt flashed across the fairy's face. But then her hand tightened around the whole bouquet. It was hers. No way was she going into service for two hundred years!

"Sorry, gang," she said as she flew with the roses toward the balcony. "I need this more than you do."

"Those are to save my parents!" cried Crystal.

"Faybelle! What trouble have you gotten into now?" Rosabella asked.

Faybelle paused. She wasn't a bad fairy. Okay, well, she was—but still, she needed to explain herself. "I need these roses to save me from a fate worse than death—hard work!"

"Think of someone else for once!" It was Daring the Beast. "This affects ever after all of us!"

Rosabella's mouth hung open. Had he changed? At last?

But Faybelle didn't listen to him. Her wings began to flutter. "That would be a *you* problem, not a *me* problem. Bye-bye!" She flew away from the palace and headed toward Ever After High.

The girls were stunned.

"How will we cure your parents?" Ashlynn wondered out loud.

"What do we do?" cried Briar.

Crystal stared after Faybelle. She was deep in thought. This was no time for despair. It was time for action. "Penguins," she commanded, "prepare the royal sleigh. We're going to follow that fairy!"

They had no time to lose.

Led by a team of royal polar bears, the Snow King's sleigh raced toward Ever After High. Everyone was crowded on board—including Daring the Beast, who was relieved not to be pulling it this time.

Faybelle reached the school castle in no time. She paused on one of the top turrets and was relieved that no one seemed to be pursuing her. She called the Fairy Mob and held up the bouquet of roses to her MirrorPhone. "Okay, I got the Roses of the Seasons."

"We'll meet you at your locker," snarled the mobster on the other end of the call. "And yes, we know where it is."

Faybelle squinted. At the edge of the horizon she saw something. It was the royal sleigh—she'd been followed after all! She ducked through a window and zipped through the snowy hallways to her locker as fast as she could.

No one was there. She looked up and down the corridor. She had no time to lose. Where were the mobsters?

"Ahem." Someone coughed—from *inside* her locker.

She spun the lock and opened the door. All three mob fairies were crammed inside. They were rummaging through her stuff.

"This color lip gloss," commented one of the mobsters, "not really working."

"Give me that," Faybelle snapped at them. "And get out of my stuff."

They flapped their wings, and Faybelle slammed the locker shut behind them. "I got the Royal Roses of the Seasons, like I promised," she said. "Old magic in exchange for my freedom."

One of the mobsters raised a bushy eyebrow. "And how do we know it's the real deal?"

Just then the front doors of the school flew open. It was

the sleigh! The polar bears were panting. The students, who had been following Blondie's reporting, poured out of the auditorium to see what was happening.

Crystal caught sight of Faybelle and ran over to her. Faybelle clutched the bouquet tightly.

"I need those roses to save my parents!" Crystal cried.

One of the mobsters leaned close to his buddy. "Um, I'm thinkin' this is legit."

Faybelle looked at the assembled students. She looked at Crystal. What was she going to do? "I need them to save myself," she whined. "I signed a deal with the mob fairies to take my detention duty to clean up the school." She wiped away a tear. "And I didn't read the fine print. Now I owe them two hundred years of service. Unless I give them these roses." She hung her head, ashamed. "I'm sorry."

Crystal felt terrible. "Oh, Faybelle."

But the mobsters were not moved by this exchange. "Boo-hoo," one of them said sarcastically. "Either we get the roses or we get two hundred years of service from you. What's it gonna be?"

Crystal forgave Faybelle. "I understand. You felt that you didn't have a choice."

"But *I* do!" Daring the Beast leaped off the sleigh. He ambled over to Faybelle and put his hands on the four roses. "Faybelle, I choose to take your place," he said nobly.

"What?" Faybelle couldn't believe her ears.

"I'll take on your debt to the Fairy Mob. You'll be free. If you give the Royal Roses of the Seasons back to Crystal."

Rosabella gasped. The other students were astonished. No one could believe that Daring could be so selfless—least of all Faybelle.

"You'd do that for me?" she asked.

"If the Fairy Mob will let me," Daring said, determined.

The head mobster shrugged. "Makes no difference who's doing the work. No sweat off our wings." He produced a contract out of thin air and handed Daring a feathered quill.

Daring signed the paper.

The mobster slapped him on the back. "Congratulations!"

The contract magically ripped apart! What was happening?

His buddy turned to the crowd. "It's in the small print," he explained. "If someone offers of their own free will to take on the work this contract is void."

"You're off the hook," the head mobster said to Faybelle.

His buddy slapped Daring on the back. "Nice job, kid. We don't see that enough these days. Okay. Fairy Mob *out*!"

They vanished. Daring handed the bouquet of roses to Crystal. "Now that that's over, we can finally—"

Daring winced. His whole body was glowing with magic. He dropped to his knees. The magic was glowing brighter and brighter. Suddenly, there was a huge flash of light—and Daring the Beast disappeared! Daring the Prince was back, and he was his old handsome self again.

"What happened?" he spluttered.

Rosabella was beaming at him. "You finally started acting like a real prince."

Daring had finally realized that the most powerful magic of all was thinking of others—and it was Rosabella who had helped him learn this lesson. He took her in his arms and gave her a great big hug. Everybody cheered.

Rosabella had finally found her prince.

CHAPTER 35

A Change in the Weather

A sleighride later, Crystal was back home. She brought the bouquet into the throne room and placed it before the Snow King and the Snow Queen. It shimmered. An enchanting fragrance filled the room. Wisps of sparkling magic encircled Crystal's parents. The ice began to thaw. The curse lifted from their eyes. They blinked, disoriented. The looked around the room sleepily.

Crystal rushed over and wrapped them both in a hug.

The Snow King rubbed his eyes sleepily. "It's like I was in a bad dream."

"But now?" asked the queen.

"But now it's over," said Crystal. She handed the staff of winter back to her father. "Dad," she told him, "we need you to stop this storm."

But the Snow King shook his head. "I've done quite enough already. Crystal, you've proven that you are ready to rule. You were always ready, but I was too snow-blind to see." He gave the scepter to Crystal.

Tears welled up in her eyes. Her father was back—and he was proud of her. She skated out to the balcony and prepared to release the wicked winter.

Blondie was broadcasting. "This just in, Ever After! Prepare yourself for a change in the weather!"

Crystal took a breath. This was big magic. She aimed the staff, and glittering ripples of pastel-colored light flowed across the land. The clouds cleared. The sun shone. The snow began to melt. Winter was over—for a little while, anyway. Crystal had saved Ever After.

Later, after all the courtiers and servants were no longer penguins and seals (except for the few who enjoyed their new forms), Crystal's parents decided it was time for a trip to the tropics. They needed a vacation. Besides, the kingdom would be just fine with Crystal in charge.

As their sleigh pulled out of the long driveway, they passed Northwind and Jackie. The two frost elves were busy shoveling snow. Lots of snow.

"Is this part of the plan, too?" Northwind asked Jackie.

"Yeah, Northwind," she said sarcastically. "Everything we did was so that we could get to do this. Fun, fun, fun."

But maybe they'd suffered enough.

Crystal raised the staff in one hand and her wand in the

other. Glittering sparkles filled the air. "I declare this a day of celebration, a day of fun..."

"A snow day!" shouted her friends happily.

"I was going to say...an epic winter!"

But it didn't really matter what she said. It was time to go sledding!